Blood on the Range

Brockley Whin arrives in Blackwater with a reputation as a gunfighter, but whose side is he on in the growing struggle between the biggest ranch, the Forked Lightning, and the smaller ranches, led by Jubal Crossan of the Circle C?

His former compadre, Amery Tasker, runs the Forked Lightning, but, much as old loyalties count, from the moment he rescues young Jeb Crossan and his girl from Tasker's gunslicks, Brockley has a tough choice to make.

Making that choice and following it through leads him to a decisive shootout before his final face-to-face encounter with Tasker and his own past.

Blood on the Range

Colin Bainbridge

A Black Horse Western

ROBERT HALE · LONDON

ISBN 978-0-7090-9967-3

Robert Hale Limited
Clerkenwell House
Clerkenwell Green
London EC1R 0HT

www.halebooks.com

Typeset by
Derek Doyle & Associates, Shaw Heath
Printed and bound in Great Britain by
CPI Antony Rowe, Chippenham and Eastbourne

CHAPTER ONE

The door of Etta's Black Cat dining parlour swung open and a man entered. Etta glanced up from the newspaper she was reading and her eyes dwelt on him. She might be worn and past her prime, but her senses could still respond. He advanced into the room and, taking a seat by the window, removed his hat to reveal dark hair which, to Etta's eyes, hung slightly long at the back. He didn't seem to notice her. Instead, he leaned forward and twitched the net curtain, giving him a view of the main street. People had gathered on the boardwalks and a large number of wagons and buggies were drawn up around the town square. He turned back and seemed to see her for the first time. She smiled and he nodded almost imperceptibly in her direction.

'What can I get you?' she asked. There was a roughly written menu on the table but he didn't appear to have seen it.

'What you got?' he said.

'Depends on what you want,' she replied. She allowed the words to stand for a moment. 'If you're hungry, I can fix up a good plate of hash with all the trimmings.'

'Sounds good,' he said. 'Throw in a pot of coffee and it'll be perfect.'

'Goes without saying,' she replied.

She went through a screened opening and the man reached into his pocket to produce a tobacco pouch. He started rolling a cigarette but then seemed to think better of it and put the pouch back again. He was looking out of the window once more when Etta appeared with a tray on which were a steaming platter of food and a coffee pot with a mug. She set it down on the table and he looked up at her.

'There's a lot of activity outside,' he said. 'Is somethin' goin' on?'

'It's easy to see you're a stranger,' she replied. 'Most everybody knows that this is the day young Jeb Crossan is goin' to carry his bride-to-be all the way to the oak grove outside of town.' The man gave her a puzzled look. 'It's kinda customary round these parts when a young couple get betrothed,' she explained. 'There's some pretty rough country and he ain't no circus strong man. A lot of folks reckon he won't make it.'

Involuntarily, her gaze fell on the stranger's broad

shoulders. Maybe it wouldn't be such a hard task for him. He looked puzzled.

'Jeb Crossan is old Jubal Crossan's boy,' she began, feeling the need for further explanation. 'Jubal owns the Circle C. Miss Willow is the daughter of Jess Giroux that runs the general store. Those two young folk have known each other since they were kids. She ain't but a chit of a thing. I figure I can see how young Jeb might have figured she'd be light enough to float, especially feeling the way he does about her, but I figure he's goin' to find it hard going.'

'Seems a strange thing to do,' the man said.

The woman laughed and her ample bosom shook. 'I guess that's just the way of it when you're young and in love,' she replied. 'It is round here. Personally, I'm bettin' that he makes it all the way.'

The man put his plate to one side and poured a second cup of coffee. 'There's plenty in the pot,' he said, 'if you'd care to join me.'

She hesitated for a moment, glancing at the empty room. 'The place is quiet,' she said. 'Everyone's out on the street. I guess it wouldn't hurt to take a breather. I'll just get another mug.' While she went for it, he pulled out a chair and when she returned he poured out the coffee, taking care not to spill any.

'That was a mighty fine meal,' he said.

'I can do you apple pie if you've got some room left.'

'Have your coffee first,' he replied.

There was silence for a moment while they both drank and then the woman spoke.

'I'm Etta,' she said, 'Etta Foy. You probably guessed that. This is my place.'

'Glad to make your acquaintance, ma'am,' he replied. 'The name's Whin, Brockley Whin.'

He held out his hand and she shook it, looking at him steadily as she did so. For a little while the talk was desultory but her curiosity was aroused. There was a lull and then she asked the question which was uppermost in her mind.

'So what brings you to this neck of the woods?' she said. 'Attendin' to some business?' He didn't reply immediately and she thought for a moment that she might have offended him. 'I'm sorry,' she added. 'Guess I've always been a mite too inquisitive.'

'Ain't nothin' to be sorry about,' he replied. 'You're right. I do have some business in these parts. Fact is, you might be able to help me. I'm lookin' for a spread called the Forked Lightning. It's owned by a man named Tasker. I understand it ain't too far from here.'

He couldn't be sure, but he had the impression that Etta almost flinched. When she looked up at him again her expression seemed to have changed. She finished off her coffee and got to her feet.

'It's been nice talkin' to you,' she said, 'but I guess

8

I'd better be gettin' back to work.'

'Ain't nobody come in,' he replied.

'There's a few things I ought to do,' she said. 'Place will likely get busy later.'

'You ain't told me how to get to the Forked Lightning,' he said.

She paused. In the unexpected silence the sounds of the street suddenly seemed loud.

'You can't miss it,' she replied. 'Just keep on ridin' due north. The trail bends east as you approach the Crossan place and eventually takes you right to the Forked Lightning. It's the biggest spread in the whole territory.'

'Much obliged,' he replied.

He got to his feet and, leaving some dollar bills on the table, walked to the door. He looked back towards the counter but Etta had gone. Putting his hat back on, he stepped out onto the boardwalk. Large crowds of people had now gathered on both sides of the street and as he moved towards the hitch-rail, a ripple of excitement seemed to pass over them. Down the street someone began to shout and then cheers rang out. He glanced in that direction. Striding purposefully down the street was a young man carrying a girl in his arms. The girl's arms were round his neck and she was laughing. The boy's face was wreathed in a sheepish grin.

'Go it, young man!' someone shouted, and the call

was taken up by various others.

'You can do it, Jeb!'

'Don't drop her! Not too far to go!'

Whin smiled. As the young couple passed, some of the people formed up behind them and followed them down the street, shouting encouragement. Stepping down from the boardwalk, Whin moved to his horse and was about to step into leather when he paused. Rather than follow directly in the path of the young man and his girl, he decided to wait till the excitement had died down. Turning away, he walked down the street till he reached the barber shop. He had been on the trail for some time. It would feel good to have a haircut, a wash and a brush-up.

When he emerged, the place was much quieter, although a number of people still lingered. Shadows had spread across one side of the street. He mounted up and began to ride slowly down the main drag. As he did so he observed that several of the stores bore the name of Tasker. There was Tasker's General Store and Emporium, Tasker's Livery and Feed, Tasker's Carpentry Shop. It seemed that, in addition to running the biggest ranch in the territory, Tasker was a big noise in town. His thoughts drifted back to the conversation he had had with Etta Foy in the dining parlour. He couldn't be mistaken. There had been an obvious reaction on her part at the mention of Tasker's name, and it wasn't a good one. The atmosphere had cooled and she had brought the talk to a fairly rapid halt. There must be a reason, but what was it?

He had left the town behind but he was almost certain that he was following in the footsteps of Jeb Crossan. He could see clear indications of the young man's footprints in the dust of the trail. He might even have surmised that the maker of the footprints was carrying something quite heavy by the way in which his feet were planted. As he rode he began to watch out for Jeb and the girl. The youngster had seemed confident enough as he came down the main street of town, but it was probably a fair way to the oak grove, even if the girl was as light as a feather. He couldn't help grinning to himself as he thought about it.

He drew his horse to a halt and looked down at the marks in the dust. If he read them aright, it seemed the young man was definitely tiring. He rode on, half expecting the single set of footprints to be joined by a second set, but it didn't happen. That young man was certainly showing some grit at sticking to his task. Maybe there had been somebody out here to observe him, but if so, there didn't appear to be anybody around any longer. His eyes swept the country. It was hilly, with tree-lined water courses in the bottoms – difficult country to be carrying a burden for any distance, even a slight young woman.

11

He was just thinking again of what an odd thing it was to attempt when his musings were cut short by a sudden rattle of gunfire.

Instinctively he dug his spurs into the buckskin mustang's flanks and rode off the trail up a long slope. He was trying to locate the direction of the gunfire when another burst of shooting rang out from in front of him. He crested the rise. Some stunted trees offered him cover and he drew the horse to a halt, his eyes scouring the landscape. At first he could see nothing but then he discerned a slight flattening of the grass leading in the direction of some rocks, above which a faint haze hung in the air. Gunsmoke! Then he saw movement and some further shots rang out. After a few moments they were answered by a single shot, which seemed to come from some low brush away to his right. In a flash of intuition he guessed what was happening. The youngster and his bride-to-be had been dry-gulched and had taken shelter in the brush. In the instant he had drawn this conclusion, he had dug his spurs into the horse's flanks and was galloping down the further slope in the direction of the rocks.

The effect of his appearance on the men concealed behind them was instantaneous as a crackle of rifle fire rang out afresh. He had drawn his own Winchester and opened fire in return, judging where the men were concealed by the puffs of smoke. He hadn't given any thought to how many men he might be up against. The only thing which rang in his head was that the boy and his girlfriend were in trouble and it was up to him to do something about it. More shots rang out from the direction of the brush and he guessed that the youngster must have opened fire in his support. The buckskin was hurtling forward at a furious pace as he bore down on the rocky outcrop. He heard the singing of lead in the air and then somebody emerged from shelter and began to sprint in the direction of the brush. Whin's finger tightened on the trigger of his Winchester and the man went down, rolling over like a felled rabbit. Whin was about to fire again when suddenly the buckskin stumbled and came crashing to the ground. He was flung from the saddle, hitting the ground hard with his head. He felt a thumping pain and everything went black.

He could have been unconscious for only a few moments because when his senses returned he could see the buckskin back on its feet not far away and he heard the sound of hoof beats. He raised his head and saw three riders heading up the hill away from him, riding hard in the general direction from which he reckoned they had come. His rifle was gone so he drew his revolver and, dragging himself up, fired a couple of parting shots in the riders' direction. A final shot came from the brush as they disappeared behind some trees. Still holding the six-gun, he staggered to his feet, feeling shaky and groggy. Apart from the pain in his head, however, he appeared to be unhurt. Presently he heard a shout and, looking towards the patch of brush, saw a young man holding a rifle in the air. As Whin acknowledged his presence, the young man turned aside and seemed to say something. In another moment a second figure rose from behind a bush. Whin was right. It was the figure of a young girl. He had come across Crossan and his bride-to-be in the nick of time. What reason anyone could have for wanting to ambush them was beyond him. The two figures emerged from cover and came forwards. He moved to the horse and quickly checked it over. It was a cursory examination but enough to assure him that the buckskin was unhurt. By the time he had finished the young pair were beside him.

'I don't know who you are, but I sure thank you for comin' to our aid just when you did,' the youngster said.

The girl was clinging to his arm and looking at Whin with a mixture of gratitude and apprehension, which made her eyes sparkle.

'I heard the shootin',' Whin replied.

The youngster's lips set in a tight line. When he opened them to speak, his features were fixed in an unexpected look of grim determination.

'Those varmints,' he muttered. 'I ain't gonna let them get away with this.'

At his words the girl looked at him pleadingly. 'Don't make matters worse,' she said. 'Let's both be thankful we've come out of it unharmed.' She turned back to Whin. 'Thanks to this man's assistance.'

Whin felt slightly awkward. In an effort to turn the conversation, he glanced up at the sky. 'It's gettin' late,' he said. 'If I'm right, we can't be too far from the Circle C ranch.'

The young man looked surprised at his words.

'I figure I know who you are,' Whin said. 'I was talkin' to Miss Etta at the café. Unless I'm way off beam, you're Jeb Crossan.' He looked at the girl. 'And you must be Miss Willow. I ain't too sure whether that's your first or second name.'

'It's my first,' she replied. 'I'm Willow Giroux.' Her eyes flickered. 'I think it's French,' she added inconsequentially.

'I'm pleased to make your acquaintance, Miss Giroux,' Whin said. 'And yours, Jeb Crossan. My name's Whin, Brockley Whin. Like I was just sayin', it's gettin' kinda late and I figure, since we're not too far from the Circle C, it might be sensible if you two were to carry on and make your way there.'

Jeb and Willow exchanged glances. 'What about you?' Jeb said. 'If you've got the time, we'd sure appreciate it if you would come to the Circle C with us. You can be sure of a good welcome.'

Whin thought for a moment. He had intended getting to Tasker's place but events seemed to be transpiring to change that. He had come upon the young couple by chance and rescued them from a difficult situation. It seemed to give them a kind of claim on his time. Besides, he was curious to know what the story was behind the incident. And there was no way of knowing that the bushwhackers might not still be around.

'That's mighty nice of you,' he said. 'I'd be obliged.'

'We ain't got no horses,' the youngster said.

'That ain't a problem. I can lead the buckskin. It's a nice evening for a walk.'

Miss Willow laughed. To Whin's ears it sounded charming, like a clear rivulet dancing over stones. 'I suppose you heard what we were doing,' she said, 'before those horrible men arrived on the scene.'

Whin smiled. 'I sure did, ma'am. And I figure if it was me instead of Jeb there, I'd have been doin' exactly the same thing.'

Young Crossan broke into a laugh too. He looked at the girl. 'I'm willin' to try carryin' you the rest of the way,' he said.

She seemed to consider it. 'There'll be plenty of time for that,' she replied. As they began to move away, Whin couldn't help thinking how composed she seemed. Considering all that had happened, it seemed to him quite remarkable that she wasn't more upset. She might be very young, he reflected, but she was certainly not silly. He sensed a toughness about her and the boy. He liked the both of them.

Dusk had fallen and it seemed to Whin that they had covered a considerable distance when they heard the approach of hoof beats. Whin's hand reached for the Winchester but the boy touched him on the arm.

'It's all right,' he said. 'It'll be some of the men from the Circle C. I thought they'd be out lookin' for us before now.'

Whin remained on his guard but the boy was right. In a few moments two riders appeared and one of them called out.

'Jeb! Willow! Are you OK?'

'We're fine. We kinda got delayed, that's all.'

The riders drew to a halt beside them and the leader peered down at Whin.

'Underwood, this is Mr Brockley Whin,' Jeb said. 'We got him to thank for helpin' us out of an awkward situation. He's our guest.'

The suspicious look on Underwood's face began to evaporate.

'Why don't Willow and I swing up behind you and Driscoll?' Jeb said.

Underwood opened his mouth as if he was about

to ask a question but then closed it and nodded. 'Git on board,' he said.

He reached down for Miss Willow and Jeb got up behind the second rider. Whin climbed into leather and they started to ride back in the direction from which the Circle C men had come. As they rode, Whin observed groups of cattle in the rapidly fading light and heard their occasional lowing. It didn't take them long to reach the ranch house. It was a solidly built one-storied building with a veranda running all the way round it. Standing outside was a buggy with a horse leaning in the traces. As they rode into the yard the door opened and a man appeared. He looked to Whin to be in his mid-forties. He stepped down to the hitch-rail as another man appeared just behind him. The second man was smaller and lighter. He ran down the steps and rushed up to Willow the moment she had dismounted.

'Willow!' he breathed. 'Thank goodness you're safe.'

'Father, I'm fine,' she said.

He held her at arm's length and then turned to Jeb. 'Willow's mother said all along that was a tom-fool prank to play,' he said.

The boy looked sheepish. 'I'm sorry, Mr Giroux. I guess I got a lot to learn.'

The other man had taken hold of Jeb by the shoulder. 'Grant's right, son,' he said, 'even if it is the custom. But hell, it's sure good to see you both.'

Jeb turned to Whin and went through the intro-ductions once more. His father shook Whin by the hand. 'Well, what are we hangin' about for?' he said. 'Let's get inside and make ourselves comfortable.' He made to climb the steps but Willow's father stopped him.

'I appreciate your offer,' he said, 'but Willow's mother will be beside herself with worry. I think we'd better get goin'.'

'Stay for a drink at least.'

Willow and her father exchanged glances. 'I think my father is right,' she said. 'I feel so guilty about having caused everyone so much trouble. We'd best be getting back to town.'

She turned and embraced Jeb, who emerged looking rather shame-faced. 'I'll be over soon,' he said.

Willow and her father stepped into the buggy. Her father pulled on the reins and the others watched as they departed in a cloud of dust.

'Mr Giroux arrived about an hour ago,' Crossan remarked. 'I ain't known him be so concerned before.'

'We didn't see him,' Jeb returned. 'I guess because we left the trail.'

'All's well that ends well,' his father said.

He led the way up the steps followed by Jeb and

Whin. Whin glanced back at the two cowboys. They were about to lead the horses to the stables. Underwood returned his look and nodded. Then he turned away. Whin followed Jeb and his father into the ranch house.

It was late in the evening. Darkness lay over the land; only the light of a kerosene lamp cast a glow on the figures of Jubal and Jeb Crossan and Brockley Whin as they sat on the veranda talking. Jubal had just refreshed their glasses from a bottle of good bourbon, which stood on a low table. Apart from the rumble of their voices, the only sounds were the soughing of the wind in the branches of some trees behind the bunkhouse and the occasional snicker of a horse from the direction of the corrals. They had eaten well but it seemed to Whin that during the course of the meal and subsequently, they had somehow avoided mentioning any of the main issues the day's events had raised but now it seemed to him that the time was right to broach the subject. He waited for an opening.

'I can't thank you enough for what you did coming to Jeb's assistance,' Jubal eventually said. 'It was sure lucky you came by when you did.'

'You've already thanked me enough,' Whin replied. 'Anybody would have done the same.'

'I don't know about that,' Jubal replied.

Whin drew on his cigarette. 'What was it all about

anyway?' he said. 'I mean, why would those varmints have wanted to dry-gulch Jeb and Willow? Have you any idea who they might be?'

Jubal shifted uncomfortably in his chair. 'Guess they were just some no-good coyotes out to cause trouble,' he replied.

Whin shrugged. 'Maybe so,' he said. 'All the same, I get a feelin' that it wasn't just accidental. Why would those varmints have been ridin' that way? There sure didn't seem to be anybody else about. I saw their sign. Thinkin' about it, it looks to me like they'd been trackin' Jeb and the girl. That wouldn't have been hard. Half the town seemed to have turned out to see them.'

'Well, even if you're right, I wouldn't want to involve you any further. You've done enough already.'

Jeb had been unusually quiet since they had come outside. Now he suddenly seemed to take an interest. 'Why try to play this down, Dad?' he said. 'I think Mr Whin deserves better.'

'That's enough,' his father replied.

The boy turned to Whin. 'My father likes to keep his business his own,' he said.

'That's fine,' Whin replied. 'I don't mean to interfere.'

Jubal exchanged glances with his son. 'Maybe Jeb's right,' he said. 'Maybe I'm gettin' old-fashioned.

What's it matter? Go ahead, you tell it to Mr Whin.'

Jeb turned to Whin. 'You're right,' he said. 'If we're honest, we can be pretty sure it was no accident.'

'It might still have been,' his father interposed.

'Sure, but it would surely be stretchin' a point. The thing is, Mr Whin, there have been a number of incidents recently and this just seems to fit the pattern.'

'What sort of incidents?' Whin said.

'Cattle have been disappearin'. The water course was contaminated. A couple of the hands got injured in so-called accidents. Then, just last week, one of them was shot and wounded quite badly. We think we know why, too.'

He paused and, taking advantage of the break, his father took up the story.'We ain't got any proof,' he said, 'but things seem to stack up. The same sort of thing has been happenin' to some of the other small ranchers around here. It's beginning to look to all of us as though someone is trying to make life difficult.'

'Why would anyone do that?'

'To get the ranchers to sell up and leave. So far the pressure has been pretty gentle, but it's building up.'

'If it's got to the stage where people have been shot and injured, it don't sound too gentle to me. Any idea who might be behind it?'

Again Jubal and Jeb exchanged glances. 'We got

22

an idea, but that's all it is,' Jeb replied.

'No one likes to spread rumours which might not even turn out to be true.'

'I can see that,' Whin replied. 'But it's OK to have suspicions.'

There was a moment or two of silence before Jubal spoke again. 'You're new around here,' he said, 'so names aren't likely to signify.'

'Go on,' Whin said.

'I don't suppose the name Tasker means anythin' to you?'

Whin was suddenly even more interested. Strangely, he was not at all surprised by what Jubal had just stated.

'Now that's a coincidence,' he said. 'It's the second time that name's come up today.'

Jubal looked up at him closely.

'Etta Foy, in the dining parlour in town,' Whin said. 'She didn't give the impression she was too fond of him either.' He didn't bother to mention that it was he who had brought the name up in the first place.

'Tasker runs the biggest spread in the area.'

'The Forked Lightning,' Whin intervened.

'Yeah, that's the one. He must have more than three thousand head of cattle. He's a big operator. But however big he's become, he ain't gonna be satisfied till he's taken over every smallholding and incorporated it into his empire. And what makes it even more galling is that he's holding thousands of acres of grazing land to which he's got no legal rights.'

'So can't somethin' be done about it?'

'He might not have the legal rights, but his money gives him a lot of leverage on the state government.'

'And apart from that, he's got plenty of heavily armed men on his payroll,' Jeb cut in.

'And you figure those varmints that bushwhacked you are some of them?'

'Either that or they were on their way to join him.'

'We reckon things are comin' to a head,' Jubal said. 'Tasker's been accusin' the small ranchers like us of takin' his cattle. OK, some of them might have been swingin' the long rope and usin' the runnin' iron, but if so it ain't nothin' like on the scale we reckon Tasker's been doin' it. Tasker's tried offerin' rewards for the arrest and conviction of so-called stock thieves, but so far he ain't got very far with that tactic. Even when he's managed to get folk into court, they've usually been acquitted by juries more in sympathy with the small ranchers. I figure he's had enough of that kind of approach. Pretty soon now, it's gonna be all-out war.'

He paused and Whin took a drink. 'If what you say is true,' he said, 'and Tasker has been gathering a regular army of gunmen, it don't look too good for you and the other small ranchers.'

Jubal shrugged but did not say anything.

'We can look after ourselves,' Jeb asserted. 'Ain't no one gonna move us off our own land.'

Whin downed the last of his drink and stubbed out his cigarette. 'Seems like a bad business,' he said.

'I didn't intend draggin' this all up,' Jubal replied. 'I'm sure you got troubles of your own.'

'Show me a man who ain't,' Whin replied. He rose slowly to his feet. 'If you gentlemen don't mind, I think I might be turnin' in.'

The other two got to their feet. 'It's been a long day all round,' Jubal said. He bent over and turned down the lamp. 'Figure it's time we all grabbed some shut-eye.'

He stood aside while Jeb and Whin made their way indoors but when they had done so he didn't immediately follow them inside. Instead he stood for a while, looking out across the pitch-dark range. Whatever his thoughts were, they were interrupted by the sound of footsteps coming from the direction of the bunkhouse; he turned his head to see the figure of his foreman materialize from the darkness.

'Underwood,' he said. 'Ain't it kinda late? I figured you'd have turned in by now.'

Underwood came up the veranda steps. 'Couldn't settle down,' he said.

'Somethin' botherin' you?' Crossan replied.

25

Underwood's gaze was directed towards the night as he leaned on the rail. 'Now you mention it, fact of the matter is there is somethin' on my mind.' He paused but Crossan didn't reply. 'It's about that new fella,' Underwood continued. 'The one came to Jeb's and Miss Willow's rescue.'

'Whin, you mean? Good job he did,' Crossan replied.

'Yeah. But I been wonderin'; what was he doin' there anyway?'

'Just happened to be ridin' through, I guess.'

'Sure, but where would he be goin'? There ain't nothin' around these parts that would be likely to interest him unless he was headin' for the Tasker spread.'

'There's no reason to think that.'

'The Forked Lightning is the only outfit in a long way that would be likely to take on someone like him.'

'Why do you say that?'

'You've seen him. I don't know what or who he is or what business he has in these parts, but it don't take much to work out he ain't no regular cowhand. We've seen some mighty mean-lookin' dudes passin' through recently on their way to join Tasker and I don't see any reason to suppose he ain't one of 'em.'

'You forget that he rescued those two young folk from what threatened to be a very nasty situation. If he had been on his way to join Tasker, why would he do that?'

In the darkness Crossan could see his foreman's shoulders hunch.

'I don't know. Maybe I got it all wrong. You've seen more of him than me. What do you think?'

Crossan walked a few paces along the veranda and then returned. 'OK, Ben, you're right. I been wonderin' myself. But like I say, he did save the lives of those young folk and I owe him.'

Underwood turned and made his way back down the steps. 'Well,' he said, 'I've told you what I think.'

'Thanks,' Crossan replied. 'I appreciate it.' He watched while his foreman disappeared round the corner of the building. When the sound of his footsteps had died away he turned and went inside the ranch house.

CHAPTER TWO

Amery Tasker was a big man; even the powerful Appaloosa on which he sat seemed somehow reduced in scale. Next to him, riding a line-back dun, was a lean, lank-haired individual known as Baltimore Johnny because of the notorious reputation he had built up all along the eastern seaboard before escaping from jail and heading west. They were accompanied by a couple of other hardcases as they looked down on a narrow valley concealed among the hills lying to the north of Tasker's spread, the Forked Lightning. Cattle were grazing but not many of them carried the Forked Lightning brand.

'Reckon it's about time we got those critters on the trail,' Tasker said.

'Whatever you say, boss,' Baltimore replied.' Guess it's gettin' kinda crowded.'

Tasker gave him an amused glance. 'Yeah, and

you're the expert on handlin' cows,' he said. Baltimore's expression was mean but in a moment it relaxed into a wolfish grin. 'Well, that's as maybe,' Tasker continued. 'What I want to know right now is how you boys got on at the Stamp Iron. I hope you enjoyed yourselves.'

Baltimore Johnny's grin broadened into a laugh. 'Sure was fun,' he said. 'I guess you won't be havin' any trouble from the Stamp Iron. In fact, I don't think there's much left of the Stamp Iron.'

Tasker was about to ask for details but decided he wasn't that interested. 'The Stamp Iron was just a practice run,' he said. 'It hardly deserves to be called a ranch.'

'Deserved,' Baltimore Johnny intervened.

It was Tasker's turn to smile. 'Whatever you say. But you won't find the Circle C or the Box W quite so easy.'

'The Stamp Iron just kinda whetted the boys' appetites,' Baltimore said. 'They're ready for more. So when do we get started?'

'All in due course,' Tasker replied. He observed the puzzled look that spread across Baltimore's face. 'Don't worry, I'll let you know real soon. I'm just waitin' for one more *hombre* to arrive. He should be here any time now.'

'You mean this fella Whin?'

Tasker's head turned quickly towards Baltimore.

'How do you know about Whin?' he snapped.

Baltimore grinned once more. 'Hell, you've mentioned his name a few times. Besides, I got talkin' to someone in town. Whin's name came up. Seems like he's one mean coyote.'

Tasker seemed to relax. 'I guess that's one way you could put it,' he said. 'Anyway, that's none of your business. Whin's an old acquaintance of mine. It'll sure be good to see him again.' He raised himself in the stirrups and let his gaze sweep across the valley. 'It's early days, but you're right about there bein' plenty of beeves down there,' he said. 'When we get back I'll have a word with Cutler about roundin' them up and changin' those brands. We'll mix 'em in with the main herd.'

He did a few quick calculations. There must be some six hundred head of rustled cattle. Add that to the legitimate herd, and he would be putting the best part of two and a half thousand head of cattle on the trail to Wichita. At, say, twenty dollars a head, that meant a big profit even after all the outlays involved. He couldn't help a thin smile from lifting the corners of his mouth. And that was only a small part of the money he meant to make once he had cleaned out the smaller ranchers. Like Baltimore had said, the Stamp Iron was just a trial run. The irony was that he was accusing the nesters of stealing cattle. That would be his excuse for dealing with them once and for all, after which he would take over the rest of the town of Blackwater and be well on the way to establishing his empire. With a nod and a word to the others, he dug in his spurs and they all began to ride back in the direction of the Forked Lightning.

Whin awoke early. He had a brief moment of confusion about his surroundings but his senses rapidly adjusted. He rose and went to the window from where he looked out on the barns and stables at the back of the ranch house. It was dark but already there was a flickering light coming from the direction of the bunkhouse. He felt a moment's guilt that he had been given such luxurious accommodation. The bunkhouse would have been fine but Jubal Crossan had insisted that he be treated as an honoured guest. It was Whin's opinion, when he had thought about it, that Jeb Crossan would probably have managed OK by himself, especially if the gunnies had been out for a bit of fun rather than seriously intending to cause mayhem. Still, with that type, there was no way of being certain. One thing he was pretty sure about, however, was that they had been on their way to the Forked Lightning. The attack on Jeb and Willow had been something of a diversion. So what did that mean in terms of himself? More to the point, what course of action was he to

31

follow now? He knew Amery Tasker from the old days; they had ridden together for a while. So when he received a message from Tasker asking him if he could do with a job working for the Forked Lightning he hadn't seen any reason not to respond. He had nothing else on hand and could do with the money. He hadn't given the matter a lot of thought – till now.

Turning away from the window, he picked up his gun-belt from where he had hung it over the bedrail, strapped it round his waist and made his way outside. There was a barrel of water beside a piece of mirror hanging outside the bunkhouse and he washed before making for the stables. The buckskin looked up at his entrance and he quickly saddled it and led it outside. He thought about leaving a note but he had no paper or pencil. He was trying to think of what he should do when the problem was solved as he heard the approach of footsteps. He glanced up; it was Underwood.

'Thinkin' of leavin' us?' he said.

'Yeah. I was wonderin' how to let Jubal know. Maybe you could tell him.'

Underwood looked at him closely. 'Yeah, I could do that. Or you could stick around a little longer and tell him yourself.'

Whin swung up into the saddle. 'I guess it don't make no difference to him either way.'

'You seem mighty anxious to be gone.'

Whin shrugged. 'Don't see no point in stayin' around.'

'Maybe Mr Crossan ain't finished thankin' you.'

'I don't want no thanks. Give my regards to Jeb and the girl, if you see her.'

'Where are you headed?'

Whin suddenly realized that he didn't know. He genuinely had no answer to the question, but instinct told him not to mention the Forked Lightning. Then suddenly he thought of Etta Foy. He realized that something about the way they had parted rankled with him, but he wouldn't have been able to say why. 'Back to town,' he said.

Underwood seemed to weigh his words for a moment. 'You could stick around the Circle C,' he said. 'If you're plannin' to stay in the area, there could be a job here. I'm Jubal Crossan's foreman. I could have a word with him.'

It was Whin's turn to consider. He was still in something of a quandary but it occurred to him that it might not be a bad idea to have something in reserve, at least till he had time to think things out properly. 'That's mighty generous of you,' he replied. 'Let me think it over.'

'Don't think about it too long. There's plenty of folk about who'd appreciate the chance of helpin' out at round-up time.'

'You're short-handed?'

Underwood smiled. 'Round-up's a busy time. It don't hurt to have cover.' His gaze suddenly fell on Whin's gun-belt. 'That's a nice set of side arms you're carryin',' he said.

Whin reached down and drew one of his guns from its holster and passed it to Underwood who looked closely at it and hefted it in his hand. 'Ain't a model I recognize,' he said.

'It's a Smith & Wesson Number 3 model,' Whin replied. 'It's new.'

Underwood handed the gun back to Whin, who replaced it in his holster and, with a nod, touched his spurs to the buckskin's flanks and rode out of the yard. Underwood watched him for a few moments before turning away. *That's a heavy weapon,* he was thinking. *A .44 calibre, a man-stopper. New. Now why would he need somethin' like that?* He himself owned a .32 model, which he had carried through the war years. He had had no use for it subsequently.

As he rode back in the direction of town, Whin took the opportunity to take a good look at the Circle C range land, which he had not been able to see the night before in the dark. It seemed strange to think that it was only the previous night he had come this way with Jeb Crossan and Miss Willow. Somehow, it already seemed like some time ago. It was a good ranch with plenty of grass and a number of streams.

Cattle grazed in little groups and they looked sleek. Assuming the other small ranches were similar, it certainly might be a temptation for some unscrupulous land-grabber to try and get his hands on them. Could what Jubal Crossan had said be true? Could Amery Tasker be that man?

Suddenly Whin stopped his musing. Even when he was deep in thought, some sixth sense was ever alert to warn him of danger. Something had triggered it now. He carried on riding, but his eyes swept the landscape all around. He could see nothing untoward but still he was uneasy. The buckskin's ears were pricked; the horse could sense something amiss also. Riding down into a wide-flowing stream, Whin saw what it was. Lying partly in and partly out of the water and trapped by a tree branch in the stream was a body. Slipping from the saddle, he waded through the water till he reached it. The man was lying on his side and there was a large gaping hole in his back where he had been shot. From what Whin could tell, he hadn't been dead for too long. He looked up and down the stream. His guess was that the man's body had been carried downstream by the fast-flowing water till it had caught on the snag. There was no sign of a horse. Reaching down, he seized the body underneath the armpits and dragged it clear of the water.

The man looked to be about forty years old. He

was wearing a close-fitting jacket and batwing chaps; the jacket was reinforced at the elbows with leather. That was enough to tell Whin that he was a cowhand who had probably been working the brush when he had been dry-gulched from behind. His thoughts reverted to the previous day's events. If this latest find was anything to go by, the attack on Jeb and Willow assumed its full import. It had not been the act of a group of roughnecks out for some fun but something much more deadly. Maybe the same group of desperados was responsible for this killing.

Whin began to drag the body further up the bank of the stream. It didn't seem right to leave it there and he was considering how he might best bury it when he was stopped in his tracks by a curt command that issued from the opposite bank.

'OK, mister. Stop right there and put your hands up!'

Whin let the body go and straightened up with his hands in the air. He heard splashing sounds behind him and soon felt the barrel of a rifle pressed against his back.

'Undo the gun-belt and let it drop.'

He did as he was ordered. When he had done so his attacker moved to one side and he had his first glimpse of him. He was a wiry figure with greying hair and skin burned to leather by the sun. As the two stood eyeing one another they heard galloping hoofs and presently another two men appeared. They slid from their saddles and came forward with their guns drawn. One of them rushed to the corpse, which lay face down, and turned it over.

'It's Mart all right?' the other man said.

The man by the corpse sprang to his feet and confronted Whin with an ugly expression. 'You dirty varmint,' he snapped. 'You're gonna hang for this.'

Whin's glance took in the two newcomers. They were both younger than the first man and they were angry.

'Let's string him up right now,' the other one said. They made a move towards Whin when the older man stopped them.

'Hold it, boys. We don't know for sure he done this. Besides, that's the way Tasker and his gang would behave. We don't want to act the same way.'

'He don't deserve nothin' else. I say he's asked for everythin' he's goin' to get.'

'And I say we take him into town and hand him over to the marshal. Let him decide.'

'That's Mart Glanton lyin' there. He's been shot in the back. What kind of low-down stinkin' coyote does somethin' like that?'

'I can see who it is,' the older man replied, 'and I feel just as bad as you about it. But there's better ways than lynchin'.'

Whin turned to the younger man. 'I didn't kill

him,' he said. 'I found him.'

The man approached and suddenly dug his rifle into the pit of Whin's stomach. 'You're a dirty liar,' he hissed. He was about to bring his rifle butt down on Whin's head when the oldster intervened. 'That's enough, Will,' he said.

The younger man looked him in the face and it seemed for a moment that they might square up to one another but after a moment he spat and turned away. The older man called to the third member of the party: 'Get his horse. We'll take him into town.'

The buckskin was standing a little distance away on the bank of the stream and it only took a few minutes for them to hoist Whin into the saddle and tie his hands to the cantle. The blow to his stomach made him feel nauseous.

'What do we do about Glanton?' the man addressed as Will said.

'Help me fasten him across my horse,' the oldster replied. 'We'll take him along with us too.'

It was getting along in the afternoon when Etta Foy, looking out of the window of the Black Cat dining parlour, saw the quartet of riders come slowly down the main street. She knew the older man. He was Chet Hoover, range boss of the Box W, and she recognized the other two as employees of the same ranch. That there had been trouble was immediately obvious by the limp figure which dangled over Hoover's horse. She couldn't make out who it was but when she looked more closely at the fourth man she was brought up with a shock. She had seen him before, and recently, but for a moment she couldn't think of who it was. Then something clicked in her memory and she recognized him as the man who had been in her café only the day before. What was his role in this? His hands were tied. Did that mean they were bringing him in because he was responsible for what had happened to the dead man? Something in her shied at the notion. Although she had only met him briefly, she had taken to him. She felt she was a good judge of character and she had sensed something solid about him. Then she recalled his query about directions to the Forked Lightning. Maybe she had been wrong. She moved quickly to the door in order to see better what was happening.

The troupe of riders drew up outside Marshal Dwayne's office where Hoover dismounted and went inside. In a few moments he emerged in conversation with the marshal. The two Box W men dismounted and together they hauled the other man from his horse and escorted him into the office. Hoover and one of the others appeared after a short time and lifted the body down from Hoover's horse and carried it inside. The door of the marshal's office closed. It certainly appeared that the man from yesterday had been brought in as a prisoner. It could only mean that he was responsible for the killing. Without realizing it, she shook her head. What was his name? She struggled to remember. It was quite distinctive – Whin, that was it, Brockley Whin. Having remembered the name, she turned back to go inside the dining parlour as the black-clad figure of the undertaker appeared down the street, heading for the marshal's office.

The first rays of dawn were coming up over the eastern horizon when Whin woke from a fitful sleep. Few of them penetrated his cell but slowly his eyes adjusted to the gloom. He glanced up at the barred opening above his head but it was too high to reach, even by standing on the iron bedstead. He moved to the cell door and peered down the short corridor but there was nothing to see. The cell opposite was empty. He returned to the bedstead and sat down on its edge. His stomach still hurt and when he pulled up his shirt to take a look there was an angry-looking bruise. He lay back and listened closely for the first sounds of movement in the street outside. Gradually the cell grew lighter; a bird called followed by another and then slowly the town began to come to life. Whin reached into his pocket for his sack of Bull Durham but it wasn't there. The marshal must have removed it. Maybe he figured Whin might try to set the building alight. Just then he heard the outer door slam; after a few moments the inner door opened and the marshal appeared carrying a tray.

'Figure you could do with somethin' to eat,' he said.

Whin became aware that he was hungry. The marshal slid the tray under the door. There was ham and eggs and a cup of black coffee.

'Compliments of Etta Foy,' the marshal said. 'I gather you've met.'

Whin dipped a slice of ham into one of the eggs and put it in his mouth. 'Sure tastes good,' he said. 'Make sure you send her my compliments.'

'Make the most of it,' the marshal replied. 'It might be a while before you get anythin' else.'

Whin looked up at him. He was short and stocky but he looked competent. 'I didn't kill that man,' Whin said. 'Like I say, I found him.'

'Yeah. That's what you say. I figure to let the judge decide that.'

'When's the judge due in town?'

The marshal shrugged. 'Could be next week, could be next month,' he said.

'I can't wait that long.'

'Seems to me you ain't got much choice.'

The marshal turned and walked away. Whin concentrated on eating his breakfast. Although it was basic fare, Etta Foy certainly knew how to cook.

When he had finished, he placed the tray on the floor and instinctively reached for his tobacco once more when he remembered that he hadn't any. He wished he had remembered to mention it to the marshal. He got up and began to walk around the cell when suddenly he heard the outer door open again. He could make out voices from the marshal's office but although he strained his ears to hear what was being said he couldn't decipher it. After all, he thought, it was unlikely to have anything to do with him. In that, however, he was wrong, because after a few minutes the inner door opened again and the marshal appeared with another person in his wake. When they got closer, Whin was surprised to see that the other man was Underwood. There was a brief glance of recognition on the part of each man and then Whin heard the jangle of keys. The marshal searched through them; when he had found the one he wanted he placed it in the door lock and turned it. There was a click and at a touch from the marshal the door swung open.

'OK, Whin,' he said. 'You can come out now.'

Whin was taken aback and didn't immediately respond.

'What are you waitin' for?' the marshal asked. Whin didn't hesitate any longer and stepped into the open.

'You got Underwood to thank,' the marshal said.

'He confirmed your story.'

Underwood nodded. 'I told the marshal what happened with Jeb and Willow and how you stayed at the Circle C. I told him what time you left.'

'Mart Glanton hadn't been killed long before you found him, but the undertaker was pretty sure it was some time before Chet Hoover arrived on the scene,' the marshal said. 'Besides, it didn't really make sense that Glanton would be on Circle C property. Your theory that he must have been carried down on the stream made some sense. The stream flows down through Box W property.'

They came through to the outer office. Whin saw his gun-belt hanging from a peg on the wall and moved towards it but the marshal stopped him.

'You might be a free man,' he said, 'but I got a policy of no firearms in town. If and when you decide to leave, you can have 'em back.'

Whin nodded. He had no argument with the marshal's rule. It seemed he kept a tight ship and Whin would have done the same.

'There's just some paperwork I got to see to,' the marshal said. 'Then you can go.'

He sat down and pulled open a drawer from which he produced a piece of paper. He was just reading through it when the door flew open and a man came through. He wore a star but to Whin's practised eye he didn't look like a lawman. It wasn't his unshaven appearance and the mean look in his eyes that made Whin think that way; it was something more subtle.

'What's goin' on, Dwayne?' he snapped.

The marshal didn't respond. Instead he carried on with the paperwork. The newcomer eyed Whin and Underwood with an undisguised look of antagonism. 'You're lettin' this *hombre* go?' he asked.

The marshal finished with the document and handed it across to Whin. 'Sign this,' he said. Whin signed. He handed the paper back to the marshal.

'OK, that's it. I may need to talk with you again. When you call back for your guns, you can let me know where I can find you.'

'I'll vouch for him,' Underwood said.

'Thanks, Marshal,' Whin said. 'I'll be seein' you.'

He and Underwood turned and walked out of the door. Whin was conscious of the deputy's eyes on his back. 'Who's that?' he asked when they were on the sidewalk.

'The deputy? He's called Lugg. I figure he's a nasty piece of work but it seems Dwayne don't have much choice. Lugg is one of Tasker's boys. You might notice Tasker's name above a lot of the properties around town.'

'I already did,' Whin remarked.

'Yeah. Tasker's got a hand in a lot of pies. It's my opinion that the townsfolk owe Marshal Dwayne a lot for keepin' a lid on things and preservin' an atmosphere of normality, but he's under some pressure.'

Whin looked up and down the street. It certainly looked normal. People were moving about, going in and out of the stores and greeting each other. A buckboard rolled past and there were horses tied to the hitch-rails. A dog ran across from one side of the street to the other.

'I reckon you and I need to have a talk about Tasker,' he said. He glanced in the direction of Etta Foy's eating house. 'How about some coffee? There's someone I got to thank for a good breakfast.'

Following his conversation with Baltimore Johnny, Amery Tasker set his range boss Nate Culver the task of rounding up the cattle. Culver had been with him a long time. He was a cowman through and through and Tasker's words came as something of a relief to him. He had recently watched the arrival at the Forked Lightning of a lot of men of quite a different stamp and he didn't like what he saw. He had his suspicions that they had been involved in some cattle-stealing and that, in addition to the main herd, there was rustled stock hidden away on grazing land to which Tasker had a questionable legal right. He didn't see it as any of his business, however, to query his boss's plans. That was Tasker's affair. He had his own duties to perform and he concentrated on doing what he had always done. So when the word came to begin

45

the roundup, he was more than happy to get on with it.

It wasn't long till Tasker, sitting on the veranda of his ranch house, began to see clouds of dust on the range, which meant that the stock was being bunched and moved towards the holding point. Things were going really well. Once the cattle were on the trail, he would be ready to put the second part of his plan into operation, and for that he required the services of Baltimore Johnny and his ilk.

The door of the Black Cat dining parlour swung open and Ben Underwood entered, followed by Brockley Whin. Etta looked up in amazement. The last person she had expected to see was Whin. At the same time she felt a stir of something inside her which was more than just surprise. While Underwood made his way to an empty table, Whin approached her. There was a warm smile on his face.

'Ma'am,' he said, 'I want to thank you for the breakfast you sent over to the jailhouse. I sure needed it.'

Etta was flustered; she struggled to regain her composure. 'I saw you yesterday evening,' she said. 'I saw them take you into the marshal's office.'

'It was all a misunderstanding,' Whin replied. 'It's been sorted out now, thanks to Underwood.'

She felt a surge of reassurance flow through her. She had felt all along that Whin couldn't have been guilty of a heinous crime . . . and yet. . . .

'Well, it's good to see you back in circulation,' she said. 'Coffee? It's on the house.'

Whin made his way over to the table where Underwood sat looking out of the window. 'You wouldn't have a cigarette?' he said. 'I forgot to ask the marshal for mine back.'

Underwood produced his pouch of tobacco. They both rolled a smoke and lit up. Etta appeared with the coffee pot and cups on a tray and placed it on the table.

'Thanks, ma'am,' Whin said.

She looked at him askance. 'No need to be so formal,' she replied. 'The name's Etta. It's right there over the door of the café.'

When she had gone Underwood turned to Whin. 'I'd say you two seem to have struck up a rapport,' he said.

Whin smiled. 'That's a fancy word,' he said. 'I'm not sure what it means.'

Underwood poured the coffee and they sat for a few moments in silence. The café was quiet. Only two couples sat at tables and after a few moments one of the couples rose from their seats and left. Having suggested to Underwood that they needed to talk, Whin felt a strange reluctance to begin the conversation. Finally, taking a deep inhalation of smoke, he broached the subject that was on both their minds.

'OK,' he said. 'What's goin' on? What's the situation with regard to this man Tasker? Jubal and Jeb told me somethin' but the picture's kinda hazy. I gather that the killing of the man whose body I found has somethin' to do with it. Chet Hoover even mentioned Tasker's name.'

'What did Jubal say?'

'Only that they suspect Tasker of runnin' off some of their beeves. He seems to think there's a lot more to it. He reckons a lot of mean, ornery characters have been makin' their way to the Forked Lightning.'

'Well, you know quite a lot,' Underwood said. 'In fact, there ain't much more that I can add. I agree with Jubal. The Circle C is a small concern. There's a few others the same, like the Box W. The man you found, Mart Glanton, was the foreman of the Box W. It's my opinion that Tasker is anglin' for some sort of confrontation with the small ranchers and that's why he's hirin' a bunch of gunslingers and desperados to do his dirty business. If I'm right, the killing of Mart Glanton is just the latest and worst example of the kind of pressure he's applyin'.'

'Like the attack on Jeb and Willow,' Whin remarked.

'Yes. And the same might have happened to them as happened to Glanton if you hadn't have come by.'

Whin thought for a moment. 'If this is right, what are the small ranchers plannin' on doin' about it?'

'Nobody's done anythin' yet. The ranchers are not the kind of folks to take up arms too easily. But the way things have degenerated, I figure they're gonna have to act real soon because things is shapin' up for a regular range war.'

'If you're right about Tasker, they aren't likely to have much of a chance.' Even as he spoke the words, he knew Underwood was right. It was clear now why Tasker had sent for him, even if there had been any reason for doubt before. Underwood was looking at him closely, as if somehow he discerned the thought in Whin's head.

'So why those guns you showed me?' he said.

'What do you mean?' Whin replied.

'I'm not stupid,' Underwood replied. 'That rig-out ain't exactly normal. I figure a man has that sort of weaponry, he knows how to use it.'

'You figure I'm one of Tasker's hired guns?'

Underwood shrugged. 'Ain't no point in me guessin',' he said, 'when you can just tell me, one way or the other.'

Whin hesitated for a moment. He took another drink of coffee. 'OK,' he replied. 'I was headin' for the Forked Lightnin'. I was answerin' a summons from Tasker. But it was pretty vague. I figured he was just helpin' me out by offerin' me a job. He didn't spell out the details. I didn't know anythin' about the situation here. I had no idea what I might be gettin' into.'

'So why would Tasker send for you? You must know the man.'

'Yeah,' Whin replied. 'I do know Tasker, assumin' this *hombre* is the same man. We first met in the war. After that we both rode for the same outfit up in the Panhandle south of the Prairie Dog River. He was just another cowhand tryin' to make a livin' in those days. After that, our ways parted. I heard he'd had a run of good luck and was doin' OK but that was all. Then I got the word to come and see him at his ranch, the Forked Lightning. I figured it was just for old times' sake.'

'That don't account for the guns,' Underwood said.

'Things went the other way for me. I hit some hard times. A man has to get by the best way he can sometimes. But I never hired out in a cause I didn't figure was right.'

Underwood was thoughtful. 'There's one good reason why I believe you.'

'Yeah? What's that.'

'If you were just another hired gun, then why would you ride against those gunslicks who tried to bushwhack Jeb and his girl? That wouldn't make no kind of sense.'

Whin thought for a moment. 'Guess I can see your point,' he said. There was another interval of silence before Underwood spoke again.

'So, that all bein' the case, what do you intend doin' now?'

Just at that moment Etta appeared from behind the counter and approached their table. 'More coffee?' she said.

Whin and Underwood exchanged glances. 'Why not?' Whin said. 'It sure seems to hit the spot.'

She went back to get fresh coffee and Whin turned back to Underwood. 'I figure I could do one of two things,' he said. 'I could just stay on here. You mentioned somethin' about a job on the Circle C.' He paused. 'Or I could carry on to the Forked Lightning and try to find out just exactly what's goin' on. Who knows, if Tasker's the same man I used to know, I might be able to do somethin' to persuade him not to attack the ranchers, if that's what he's got in mind. At the least I might be able to get some inside information that might be helpful to our cause.'

'Wouldn't that be a mite dangerous?' Underwood said. 'What if any of those varmints who attacked Jeb and Willow recognize you?'

Whin considered his comment. 'I don't think that's likely,' he said.

Underwood didn't reply, but he had noticed the way in which Whin had used the expression 'our cause'. Before Etta had returned with the coffee Whin had made his decision.

'I figure I'll carry on to the Forked Lightning,' he

51

said. 'I might be of more use that way. Besides, I ain't seen Tasker in a long time. I'm kinda curious to see how things are with him.'

CHAPTER THREE

Whin was on Forked Lightning property a long time before he realized it. He had expected to see cattle and since there were none he assumed he had not yet arrived. Then the trail he was following came to a halt at a large barred gate with a sign above it showing a jagged slashed line. He brought the buckskin to a halt and at the same moment felt a crump of air followed by the boom of a rifle. Instantly he dropped from the saddle and, rolling to one side, took what shelter he could behind the gatepost. He drew the Smith & Wesson which he had retrieved and looked around for any sign of his attacker. There was nothing to be seen, not even a whiff of smoke, but at some little distance beyond the gate there was a patch of brush which might offer cover to his assailant. He was concentrating his attention on it when he was surprised to see, out of the corner of his eye, a horse and rider appear from a different direction altogether. The rider had replaced his rifle in its scabbard and as he rode forward he gave no indication of any concern for his own safety. The rider obviously knew that Whin was sheltering behind the gatepost so, reckoning there was no point in trying to remain concealed, Whin stood up and placed his own gun in its holster. In a few moments it became clear why the rider was unconcerned: following in his wake two more horsemen appeared. As the first rider got close, Whin got a clear view of him. He was lean and his long hair streamed behind him in the breeze. He brought the line-back dun to a halt in front of Whin.

'You're takin' big chances, stranger,' he said.

'I'd say that's a mighty unfriendly attitude,' Whin replied.

'You're on private range. That was just a warnin'.'

The other two riders had drawn up beside the first man. They were observing Whin closely, taking notice of the guns he carried.

'I got business,' Whin replied. 'You might say I'm here by invitation.'

One of the other two riders turned to the first man. 'Could be he's come to join in the fun, Johnny,' he said.

Without waiting further, Whin caught the reins of his horse. 'I'm kinda tired with this,' he said. 'I'm here to see Amery Tasker. I suggest you take me to him right now.'

The man addressed as Johnny gave Whin a hard, searching look. 'You'd better be right about this,' he said. He reached down and opened the gate before signalling for Whin to fall into line behind the others; with Johnny bringing up the rear, they moved forward. Whin was conscious that Johnny had drawn his rifle from its scabbard and that it was pointed at his back but he wasn't too concerned. It was a fact that he was there at Tasker's invitation. He figured the whole episode had been more for show, but all the same it said something about Tasker's attitude and the set-up at the Forked Lightning. It was a hostile atmosphere he was riding into. He had to remind himself that, at least from Tasker's perspective, he was expected to be part and parcel of it.

Whin had expected the ride to be very short but they kept on going. He began to have some idea of the scale of Tasker's operation and when they finally came in sight of the ranch house he was impressed by the scale of it. It was no ordinary building and Whin could immediately discern signs of wealth and affluence. It was long and low with a patio and garden and several outhouses. Trees had been planted at the back and around the sides of the building to provide shelter and protection and there was a reed-fringed pool of water shaded by drooping willows. Some distance away there were corrals and off to the right stood a windmill with revolving vanes slicing the air.

'Nice spread,' Whin remarked.

There was no reply from the other three as they carried on riding into the spacious yard. As they drew to a halt, the door to the ranch was flung open and Amery Tasker appeared. He looked from one to the other of his henchmen and last of all his gaze fell on Whin. He carried on staring at him for a few moments till a light of recognition dawned in his eyes.

'Brockley Whin!' he exclaimed. 'You old son-of-a-gun.' His glance returned to the man called Johnny who was still holding the rifle. 'What the hell are you doin'?' he said. 'Put that rifle away.'

Johnny hesitated for a moment and then slid the rifle back into its scabbard. Tasker now observed for the first time that Whin's hands were fastened to the saddle-horn.

'Get down from that horse and undo his wrists quick.'

Johnny slid from the saddle but he delayed just long enough so that it was the other two who carried out Tasker's orders. Whin climbed down and began to rub his wrists.

'Take the horses and see they're looked after,' Tasker snapped. 'Baltimore, I want to see you later.'

Baltimore Johnny turned to Whin; the scowl on

his face was like thunder. Then the three of them started to lead the horses in the direction of the stables.

Tasker rushed down the steps. 'I can only apologize for what seems to have happened,' he said. 'I'm afraid that Baltimore gets ahead of himself sometimes. He's certainly exceeded any instructions I gave him; or any of the others, for that matter.'

'Baltimore,' Whin said. 'Well, his behaviour makes sense if that's Baltimore Johnny.'

'You've come across him?' Tasker said.

'Heard the name. I understand he's built up quite a reputation back East.'

Tasker put his arm around Whin's shoulder. 'Never mind all that now,' he said. 'Baltimore may have a bad reputation, but he has his uses. Right now we got a lot of catchin' up to do. Come on in. I figure you could use a strong drink. While we're enjoyin it, I'll get the cook to rustle us up somethin' real tasty.' He looked at his old acquaintance again. 'Brockley Whin! Well, I'll be! You ain't even changed much.'

They walked together up the porch steps and through the ranch house door. All the while Whin had been observing his host. He hadn't changed a lot either from how he remembered him. He had put on some weight and his hair was greying but that was to be expected. Essentially he seemed the same, but nonetheless Whin felt that there was something subtly different about him. He could not have said what it was, but it was there. It was too early to come to any conclusions. They had just met, the first time in a long while. Give it a bit of time and maybe whatever it was it would become a whole lot clearer.

The day that Underwood got Brockley Whin freed from the jailhouse, young Jeb Crossan followed him into Blackwater. Avoiding the main street of town, he made his way to Giroux's house, which was set among some trees a few streets back from where he ran his general store. Fastening his horse to the picket fence, he had just entered the garden when from round a corner of the house where she had been pegging out some washing, Willow appeared. They ran into each other's arms and Jeb held her closely for a few moments.

'Are you OK?' he whispered. 'I mean, after what happened and everything?'

She looked up at him and though her eyes were damp with tears, there was a warm smile on her face. 'Yes, especially now you've come.'

He glanced up at the house. 'Are your mother and father at home?'

'Father is at the store. Mother is resting. You know she's not a strong woman. I think the whole thing upset her more than any of the rest of us.'

'Can you leave her for a little while? I want to talk to you.'

She gave him an anxious look but the expression on his face quickly assured her. 'She was asleep the last time I looked in on her. I won't disturb her just yet. I'm sure she'll be all right for a while.'

She slipped her arm through his and then, without needing to take thought, they began to walk down the side of the house from which she had emerged. The way led across the garden and through a small orchard to a track at the bottom, which led through a grove of trees towards the lake that had given the town its name. Neither of them spoke till they came out on its banks. The lake was encircled and shaded by trees which served to give the waters their deep colour. At one point a small dilapidated jetty ran out into the lake; it was one of their favourite trysting places. When they had reached it, Willow looked up at Jeb.

'What was it you wanted to say?' she said. 'You are being a little mysterious.'

Jeb smiled at her. 'It's quite simple, really,' he said. He hesitated, suddenly feeling gauche. 'I don't know any fancy way of puttin' things. I ain't much use with words so I reckon I'd best just say it. The fact is, I don't want to wait any longer to get married. I want us to marry soon, as soon as we can. I knew we said we would wait till we were older and I was in a better position to take over the running of the Circle C. I know your parents think we shouldn't rush things and I'm sure that from their point of view there are good reasons to delay. But we know how we feel.'

Willow took his hand. 'Are you saying this because of what happened the day before yesterday?' she said.

Jeb thought for a moment. 'I ain't denyin' that it has somethin' to do with it,' he said. 'But I been thinkin' about it for a whiles now. I guess that just kinda brought things to a head. After all, there's folks just as young as us get married, so why shouldn't we?'

Willow's eyes wandered over the lake. The sun was high and streaming down over the treetops so the waters looked blue and inviting. 'I really don't know why they call it Blackwater,' she said inconsequentially.

His eyes followed hers. 'It sure looks nice today,' he said.

Suddenly she turned to him and buried her head on his chest. He reached down and raised her face towards his. 'What do you think?' he said. 'Do you think . . . I mean, could you. . . ?'

'Of course,' she replied. 'I feel the same way. I want to be married to you, I want to be your wife.'

He held her close and neither of them said anything further for a time. Finally she drew away from him. 'Of course, I'll have to have the support of my parents, and you'll have to tell your father. How do you think he'll feel about it?'

Jeb grinned in a boyish way. 'Don't worry about my dad,' he said. 'I figure there won't be any opposition from him. He thinks almost as much of you as I do.' He paused. 'Not in the same way, of course,' he added awkwardly.

Willow laughed. 'I hope not,' she said. Again they were silent till Jeb asked: 'When will you mention it? Will you take it up with them or should I make an approach?'

She looked across the lake again, thinking hard, before turning back to him. 'I don't know. I need to think. I don't suppose there'll be any serious opposition, but they have their own views. Perhaps it'll be best if I approach them gently, maybe have a word with Mother first. I don't know. You'll need to speak with them soon, but leave it with me for now,' she concluded.

They began to walk away, retracing their steps. Jeb felt as though he were walking on air. He was so buoyant; there was no weight that could bear him down.

It was growing late as Tasker and Whin sat together, each enjoying a good cigar. Whin could have no complaints about Tasker's hospitality but he had been careful about how much of Tasker's whiskey he had drunk. Tasker, on the other hand, had drunk a lot and was in a relaxed and talkative state of mind.

'You seem to be doin' well,' Whin prompted.

Taker laughed. 'I guess I got no reason to complain,' he said. His threw out his hand in a sweeping motion which included the room, the ranch, the open range beyond. 'Hell, this is nothin'. It's only the start. I got plans. And you're welcome to get right on board.'

'Sure. I guess you didn't send for me for nothin', though.'

'Let's just say it was for old times' sake.' Whin realized that Tasker was using the same words he had used when talking with Underwood. Tasker took another swig of whiskey.

'OK,' he continued. 'You're right. That wasn't the only reason I got in touch with you. And let me tell you, it wasn't easy to track you down. Fact of the matter is, some obstacles standin' in my way are gonna need a bit of persuasion to move aside. It won't hurt to have some backup. You were always pretty useful with a gun. I've heard stories that say you're even better than you used to be. I asked a few questions. From the answers I got, I figured you might be the sort who could appreciate a real opportunity. Like I say, I got big plans. Just a little push now and I'll really be on my way; yeah, all the way to Washington. And when I really hit the big time I won't forget anyone who's helped me along the way.'

'Obstacles, you say. What kind of obstacles?'

'A bunch of settlers and nesters. The West ain't got no use for those kind of folks any more. They're nothin' but a hindrance to the way of progress. Most of 'em ain't nothin' but rustlers anyway. They got a few smallholdings and no capital. I've offered them good money to quit, but they're stubborn. Trouble is, they elect the political officials. So it's come to the point where the only alternative I got is to drive 'em out by force. They've left me no choice.'

'How many of these settlers are involved?'

'There's a few, but most of the opposition has come from two small spreads, the Circle C and the Box W. They might be able to attract a few others to their cause, but once they've been dealt with the rest will just fade away.'

'How many men you got?'

'I got plenty cowhands, but I figured they weren't the type of men I needed. So I got about twenty hard-cases to do the job. The leaven in the lump, you might say. Some of the stockmen will back them up.'

'Anyone I might know?'

'Apart from Baltimore Johnny? I don't know. You'll meet 'em soon enough.'

Whin put the cigar to his mouth and inhaled. As

he blew out smoke he reached for his glass and took a sip.

'Sounds like you got everythin' in hand,' Whin said. 'So when do you figure on ridin' against the Circle C and the Box W?'

'I was just waitin' for you to arrive,' Tasker said. 'Now you're here, there ain't no reason to wait. I got a herd of cattle about to start down the trail. Once they're on their way, we move against the nesters. Let's say in two, maybe three days' time.'

Whin was thinking rapidly, although he did his best to preserve an outward air of calm to Tasker. 'Funny,' he said. 'I didn't see any cattle on the way in.'

Tasker tapped the side of his nose. 'That's because there ain't no cattle on the range. They've been rounded up and are being kept in a private place. Let's just say I own a lot of land and not all of it official Forked Lightning property.'

Whin recalled Crossan's words about suspecting Tasker of holding many acres of grazing land to which his legal rights were, at best, dubious. No doubt one of the tasks of the desperados he had been hiring was to look after things there.

'So what do you reckon?' Tasker concluded. 'Are you in? Hell, I guess I don't even need to ask you that.'

'Sure. I'm in,' Whin replied.

'Just make yourself comfortable; familiarize yourself with the set-up. I'll take you over to the bunkhouse in the morning and you can meet the boys who are still around. Like I say, some of 'em have been helpin' out with the round-up but they'll be back soon. And in two days we ride.'

It was late when Marshal Dwayne stepped out of his office. He had been catching up on some paperwork and dusk had fallen when he finally took his leave. It was a short walk to his house but he decided to take a longer way round and enjoy the cool of the evening. The streets were deserted now but from the doors of the Diamondback saloon the tinkling of a piano could be heard. As he came abreast of it the batwings suddenly flew open and a man appeared on the boardwalk.

'Dwayne!' the man shouted. 'I got some business with you.'

Dwayne halted. The man was dressed in a frock-coat which was thrown aside to give easy access to the guns slung around his waist. Behind came another man, shorter than the first but with the same mean look across his unshaven features. Dwayne observed them closely, weighing up angles and deciding which to go for first should it come to a showdown.

'You hear me, Dwayne? I said I got business with you and I aim to settle it right here and right now!'

Still Dwayne remained silent as the two men stepped off the boards and walked slowly towards him. Catching sight of the badge fixed to Dwayne's chest, the first man halted while the second came alongside and then moved slowly to the right of his partner.

'That badge don't impress me none,' the first man continued.

It had become apparent to Dwayne that there was no way to avoid a confrontation and he had worked out which man he was going to aim for first. While the man in the frock-coat was talking, the other man's hand had moved closer to the handle of his gun and was hovering nervously now in the air just above it. Dwayne noticed he had a crosswise draw. It might slow him momentarily but they both looked like accomplished gunslingers, men who made their way by the gun.

'You made a big mistake, Dwayne, lettin' that varmint go.'

Dwayne didn't know what was going on, but he guessed the man was referring to Brockley Whin. But what had they to do with it? How did they even know who he was or that he had been set free?

'Do you hear me, Dwayne? You're goin' to die like a dog, like the dirty dog you are. Do you hear me?'

Dwayne was watching the man's eyes for any flicker which might indicate that he was about to draw when, in his peripheral vision, he saw the other man's hand suddenly drop towards his gun. Almost instantly his own .45 was in his hand and spitting lead. The man reeled backwards and in the same moment Dwayne dropped to one knee and, taking the barest moment to steady himself, fired again. Two guns exploded in the same instant but it was the man in the frock-coat who lurched back, blood pouring from a hole in his chest. Gathering up all his strength he succeeded in steadying himself but as he fired once more, Dwayne's final bullet smashed into his face. Still he managed to stay upright for a second or two; then he crashed to the ground like a felled tree and lay motionless in the dirt. Dwayne turned to the other man. He was lying flat on his back, twitching spasmodically. Getting to his feet again, Dwayne walked over to where he lay. The man's face wore a look of surprise but the eyes were blank pools of nothingness and with a final shudder he stiffened and died. Dwayne looked up and down the street. It was still deserted but the doors of the saloon sprang open, spilling a few of its inmates onto the boardwalk.

'Get Doc Smith!' somebody shouted. Another man came over to where Dwayne stood.

'Better get the undertaker,' Dwayne said.

More people were running towards the scene and at the back of them Dwayne saw the figure of the deputy marshal, Lugg. He came forward through the gathering crowd.

'OK, folks,' he shouted. 'Show's over. Get back off the street.' Reluctantly people began to move away.

'They gave me no choice,' Dwayne said. He knelt down and examined the bodies.

'A couple of no-good gun-totin' polecats,' Lugg said over his shoulder.

A number of spectators still remained, although it was dark and lights had appeared in some of the windows.

'OK, everyone. There's nothin' else to see. Better get on back to your homes,' Dwayne called.

As they moved away the undertaker's wagon appeared; Dwayne and Lugg helped load the bodies on board. When they had finished and the wagon began to drive off down the street, Dwayne turned to his deputy.

'I ain't sure just who those gunnies were,' he said, 'but they seemed to know somethin' about that fellow Whin.'

It was hard to see Lugg's features in the gloom. 'I guess they must have seen him bein' taken in. Maybe they got some connection with the Box W,' he said.

Dwayne thought for a moment. 'I don't think so,' he replied. 'I know most of those Box W boys and these were different.'

The deputy shrugged. 'Who knows?' he said.

Dwayne wasn't in a frame of mind to pursue the matter. 'Well, it ain't the kind of trouble we usually get in Blackwater,' he said. 'Let's hope it ain't the start of somethin'.'

With a nod he turned away. As he walked he was aware of Lugg's eyes on his back. What was he doing out so late? Dwayne thought. Was it a coincidence that he had appeared just when he did? He hadn't wanted to take Lugg on as a deputy. There had been a certain amount of pressure from the town committee for him to do so and he had done it reluctantly. And Lugg had made no secret of the fact that he had once been employed by the Forked Lightning. Another thought occurred to him. Whatever lay behind the incident, the gunnies had challenged him to the fight. The next time, if there was a next time, there might be no challenge: just a hail of lead from some bushwhacker down a side alley. He would need to be on his guard.

For the second time in almost as many days, Whin woke up in a bed with fresh linen sheets. He had been prepared to take his place in the bunkhouse but Tasker had insisted on him taking a spare room in the ranch house. He probably had a few to spare. A washbowl and towel had been provided. As he washed he heard the sound of horses' hoofs and glanced outside to see two riders making their way to the stables. Something about them seemed familiar but he put the thought out of his mind. He returned to his ablutions but before long he heard the sound of footsteps climbing the porch steps. There was a knock; in a few moments the door was opened and whoever it was went inside. The sound of voices reached him up the stairs. Whin felt uneasy. It was early for anyone to be wanting to see Tasker. Something was troubling his mind and then suddenly he had an intuition about where he had seen the riders before. One of them was wearing a distinctive red shirt, but more than that, it was the horses they were riding. They looked like the ones the gunnies who had attacked Jeb and Willow were riding. If he recognized their horses, they would probably recognize his buckskin, which was in the stables. He thought rapidly. The fact that he had shot it out with them might not necessarily be very damning. It proved nothing about Whin or his intentions either way. All the same, it was awkward. Whin had heard enough the night before to apprise him of the situation. He wasn't likely to learn a lot more by sticking around. Tasker had already mentioned that the cattle herd was almost ready for the trail drive. He didn't know exactly where it was, but he had already been thinking that it might be worth taking a look out that way. In a flash his mind was made up. He fastened his gun-belt and strode to the window.

The room was one floor above the ground but it faced onto the front. Quickly, he turned and made for the door. He opened it slowly and glided through. Silent as a shadow he crossed the landing to the room opposite. He had no way of knowing whether or not it was occupied but he decided to take the chance. He put his hand on the doorknob and turned it. The door opened and he slipped inside. The room was smaller than the one he had been given and it was empty. He crossed to the window and raised the sash. It opened on a patch of open ground leading to the lake but it was only a short distance to the stables. He climbed over the window ledge and lowered himself so he was hanging by his fingertips. There was still a decent drop; bracing himself, he released his hold and fell to the ground, rolling over on impact.

It was a jarring fall but he was unhurt. Quickly he doubled over and ran for the entrance to the stables. The place was empty but some of the horses were restless. It took him only a matter of seconds to locate the buckskin. There were saddles hanging on the stable wall. He flung one over the back of the horse and led it to the runway at the back of the stable. He paused to glance round but it was early and none of the hands seemed to be around. He led the horse round the side of a deserted corral before stepping into leather. He applied his spurs and in a few moments entered a grove of trees. He paused in their shelter for just a few moments while he gave a final thought as to which way he should go. He could veer round and try and get back on the trail which led to Blackwater. He considered the option but decided against it. Instead, he would follow his instinct and locate the herd. It was a fair bet that it would be somewhere in the rougher high country he had glimpsed from the bedroom window. He rode forward, halting at the edge of the trees to ascertain that the coast was clear, before spurring the buckskin to a gallop. The ranch house was soon left behind, but he had a feeling that it wouldn't be too long before Tasker would be on his trail and looking for an explanation.

CHAPTER FOUR

After getting back to his house, Marshal Dwayne sat up late thinking over what had happened. It was a long time since something like that had occurred in Blackwater. Taken together with the killing of Mart Glanton and the attack on Jeb Crossan and Willow Giroux, it formed an unwanted and sinister pattern. The fact that all three events had occurred so closely together could be no coincidence. He was aware also of the concerns that the Circle C and Box W spreads had about the pressures that were being put upon them and that the man they suspected of being behind those pressures was Amery Tasker. Dwayne could sympathize with their feelings because he felt the same way with regard to his position as town marshal. Tasker's Forked Lightning spread was the biggest in the area and his influence on the town of Blackwater was becoming more and more insidious.

It was due to his influence that Lugg had been given the position of deputy marshal and Dwayne was under no illusions that it would suit Tasker to have him removed from office. The more he thought about it, the more it seemed like Tasker might be behind the gunnies too. He didn't see how they could have known about Brockley Whin unless the deputy marshal had told them. The pieces of the puzzle seemed, increasingly, to fit. But if all that was true and his reasoning was correct, what was Tasker's game? And of more immediate importance; what was his next move likely to be? It seemed to Dwayne that a trip to the Circle C and the Box W was urgently needed to talk things over.

Whin rode hard till he was well clear of the ranch. His subsequent progress was easy because he soon picked up the trails which had been left by the cattle. He slowed the horse down to its own pace in order to conserve its energy and as he rode his eyes swept the horizon in case any of Tasker's men should appear. Some of them would have been assigned to combing out the draws and coulees and could still be at the task. As he rode into the foothills, he was even more alert. There were plenty of places where a man might be concealed and he listened closely for any tell-tale sounds that might betray where men were still working, getting any wild stock out of the breaks. The day grew hot and flies were a constant menace to both himself and the horse, but the buckskin was mustang-bred and made good progress over the rough terrain.

They were climbing higher and the slopes were dotted with spruce and pine. The trail began to wind and twist through a notch and then opened out to reveal a long grassy valley hemmed in by hills. The cattle were there, and there were plenty of them. He drew the buckskin to a halt and reached for his field glasses. From what he could see, the gather seemed to be about complete. The herd was mostly bunched up; now and again some of the cows would start to move out but they were soon driven back by one of the cowhands. There were pens where branding was still going on. Plumes of smoke rose from the fires. There seemed to be no shortage of men for the job. The wind was blowing from Whin's back but despite the distance still remaining between him and them, he could hear the bawling of the cows and the occasional shouts from the men. He fancied he could smell the aroma of burned hide and hair. He had plenty of experience with cattle and it was clear to him that the herd was about ready to be moved out. What was less clear to him was what he should do next. He began to think that maybe he would have done better to get back to Blackwater and the Circle C; he could still do that but having come this far and located the herd, it seemed pointless to just ride away again. He figured that Tasker would have his men out looking for him in that direction. Sooner or later they would come this way but he wasn't too concerned. The same circumstances which had caused him to be careful on his ride here now operated in his favour. There was plenty of cover. It would be hard for anyone seeking him to find him in this terrain and he was confident of his own ability to make himself scarce. So what could he do to frustrate Tasker?

In a flash the answer came to him. It wasn't difficult: in fact it was obvious. He would wait till the herd was on the move and then see what he could do to create a stampede. At the very least it would cause some minor disruption to Tasker's plans. Men would be occupied in rounding up the herd and it might delay Tasker's assault on the small ranchers. Not all of his gunslicks remained at the Forked Lightning; some of them were no doubt involved with the round-up. He couldn't be sure whether it was a good plan or not but he determined at least to wait and see what happened. To some extent it depended on whether the herd would be moving out soon, and that seemed more than likely.

Things turned out very conveniently for Marshal Dwayne, because when he arrived at the Circle C it was to find that Joe Dunlop, the owner of the Box W, had arrived just before him. Jubal Crosan seemed especially keen to welcome him, and the reason became clear when the three men sat down together.

'Joe and me were just thinkin' about you,' Crossan said.

'Yeah? I'd have thought you might have more important things on your minds.'

'We have things on our minds, that's for sure,' Dunlop said, 'but they concern you too, Marshal. Leastways that's the way it seems to us.'

Crossan turned to Dwayne. 'Let me ask you what you're doin' here,' he said. 'I figure there's a connection. It ain't a coincidence that we're all here together, and my hunch is that it all comes down to the same thing.'

'OK,' Dwayne replied. He went on to tell them about what had happened the previous evening. 'I got to thinkin' about it and about some of the things you folk have been tellin' me,' he said, 'and I came to the conclusion that we need to do somethin' quick before things get really out of hand.'

'You mean do somethin' about Amery Tasker,' Dunlop said. 'Because I think we all know that Tasker is behind all our troubles.'

Dwayne was about to say something to the effect that there was no real proof of this, but as soon as he opened his mouth he knew it wasn't true. He would have been saying, not a truth, but a platitude.

'Dwayne's right about things gettin' out of hand,'

Crossan said. 'This whole affair started with some of our cattle bein' rustled. Now Mart Glanton has been murdered, my son and his bride-to-be only just escaped with their lives, and it seems the gunnies are takin' their violence right into town.' He paused and turned to the marshal. 'My foreman, Ben Underwood, said something about Brockley Whin takin' off to the Forked Lightning. Seems like he once knew Tasker and got a message to ride out there. That would seem to confirm what we guessed all along, that Tasker is gatherin' a whole nest of gunnies to carry out whatever dirty work he's got in mind.'

'You let this man Whin go,' Dunlop said. 'In view of what Jubal has just said, I hope you did the right thing.'

'Underwood is willin' to vouch for Whin,' Crossan said. 'And after what he did to rescue Jeb and Willow, I'm prepared to vouch for him too.'

'So why's he gone to the Forked Lightnin'?' Dunlop said.

'Whatever he hopes to achieve, he's on our side,' Crossan replied.

The marshal's brow was creased in thought. 'Whatever this fellow Whin's game is,' he said, 'I think Jubal's right about Tasker's surroundin' himself with a bunch of hardcases. He ain't doin' it for fun, so I figure that means we could be in for a range war any time now. I think we all need to do somethin' about gettin' ourselves prepared and we can't afford to waste any more time. What about the ranch-hands? How much do they know about what's goin' on?'

'I think they got a pretty good idea,' Dunlop said. 'Especially after what happened to Mart Glanton. I know that Hoover and the other two boys that were with him are just burnin' to take their revenge.'

'Then call a meetin' of the hands; tell 'em to get ready for what's comin'. How do you figure they'll take the news?'

'They signed to the brand. They'll do whatever it takes. I ain't got no worries on that score,' Dunlop replied.

'Me neither,' said Crossan. 'Whatever Tasker's got in mind, we'll be ready for it.'

When they had finished talking and as Dwayne was riding away, he was feeling a lot better. Tasker wasn't likely to have it all his own way. The small ranchers would be prepared. They might be outnumbered and they might have to face a horde of hardened gunslicks, but they would put up a show. Thinking of it, he drew his horse to a halt. He had intended riding straight back to town, but thought it might be worth calling on the Stamp Iron while he was about this business. The Stamp Iron was a very small concern but old Matt Borg who ran it was likely to be involved too. He touched his spurs to his horse's flanks and began to ride towards the ranch.

He covered the miles at a steady lope; after the incident with the gunnies and his suspicions about Lugg, he kept a careful watch for any signs of danger. At one point he came upon a loose horse grazing, still saddled, and soon there were plenty of indications of riders having passed that way. When he reached the boundaries of the property it was to find the wire fence breached in several places and in part completely torn down for some distance along the line. Dwayne continued to ride parallel to the fence and it wasn't long before he found evidence of a struggle in the form of bodies lying in the grass. Getting down from his mount to examine them, he came to the conclusion that they were some of the Stamp Iron hands. Turning his horse, he stepped it over the remnants of the wire.

A short distance beyond he found a few longhorns which had been shot and lay, like their human counterparts, gathering flies. The scents of the range filled his nostrils but as he got nearer to the Stamp Iron ranch house they were mingled with another more acrid smell, the smell of stale smoke and ash. He quickened the horse's pace, fearful of what awaited him but anxious to find out. As he topped the long rise overlooking the ranch house his heart was pounding but he already knew what he would find. Down below him, the place lay in ruins, wisps and plumes of smoke still rising from the fire-blackened remains. His horse's ears were pricked and it seemed reluctant to walk down the slope leading to the yard. There was another smell that was bothering it: the smell of charred flesh. Pulling his bandanna up to his eyes, Dwayne urged the horse forward. As he approached the smouldering embers he could see bodies lying in various contorted positions, some of them burnt beyond recognition. The only part of the structure that still partly remained was the outbuilding which had been connected to the main ranch house by a covered passage, it too having collapsed in on itself.

Dwayne dismounted, hobbled his horse and drew his rifle from its scabbard. With his eyes open for any sign of trouble, he proceeded on foot to examine what was left of the Stamp Iron. It was obvious that a major conflict had taken place there and the defenders seemed to have put up a good fight. He assumed that most of the bodies clustered about the ruins of the ranch house were those of Stamp Iron men who had been pinned down there, but what about the bodies which were lying any distance away? It was a grim scene. The outbuildings had been destroyed, some wholly and some partially. Moving away from the house, Dwayne soon discovered evidence that a lot of riders had made off in the direction of the hills.

A section of the bunkhouse still stood and Dwayne made his way towards it, his rifle at the ready, eyes and ears strained for anything untoward. He had seen no signs of activity, just dead and burnt bodies, but as he approached the bunkhouse he thought he heard a movement.

He tensed and slid behind an angle of the one remaining scarred and blasted bunkhouse wall. Flattening himself against it so as to make himself as invisible to anyone inside as possible, he listened intently for any repetition of the sound. There was nothing, just the buzz of flies and the gentle soughing of the wind. Maybe it had been a rat or some other creature moving through the ruins. It couldn't be long before the coyotes arrived; high overhead, buzzards were already circulating. For what seemed a long time he remained in the same position and had just about decided that he had been mistaken when there came another sound, and this time there could be no mistake. It was the sound of a gun being cocked. Dwayne raised his own rifle and began to move stealthily backwards. There were further sounds from within the building which sounded like muffled footsteps. Whoever was inside was moving towards the gaping hole which formed the entrance to the ruined bunkhouse. Dwayne halted once more, scarcely breathing, waiting for the person within to show himself. The seconds ticked by. A hand appeared carrying a gun and then an arm and shoulder. Dwayne decided the time had come to act.

'Drop the gun!' he shouted. 'I got you covered.'

There was a moment's hesitation and then whoever was inside the building threw the gun to one side.

'Come on out!' Dwayne barked. 'All the way out. And remember there's a Henry rifle pointing right at you.' Slowly the man advanced into the open, his back to the marshal.

'OK, turn round!'

The man obeyed, moving very deliberately, until he was side-on to Dwayne.

'Matt!' Dwayne gasped. 'Matt Borg!'

The man completed his revolution and looked at Dwayne with a mixture of surprise and relief spread across his countenance. 'Marshal Dwayne,' he said and then confusedly: 'What are you doin' here?'

Dwayne let the rifle drop so that its muzzle was facing the ground. He was about to reply when he noticed that blood was flowing from a wound in Borg's upper arm. 'Looks like you could do with some treatment,' he said.

Borg didn't argue 'I've lost a lot of blood,' he replied. 'I think I must have passed out.'

The next moment he had suited action to the words. A glazed look passed across his eyes and without further ado his legs gave way beneath him

83

and he slid, almost gracefully, to the ground. Dwayne walked across to his horse and pulled some items out of his war bag together with a canteen of water and a flask containing whiskey. Lifting the fallen man's head, he attempted to pour some whiskey down his throat but Borg was out cold and the whiskey just ran from the corners of his mouth. Tearing aside what was left of Borg's shirt, Dwayne first washed the wound and then doused it with more whiskey. One look told him that though it was a nasty injury it was not likely to be life-threatening. The bullet had passed clean through the flesh below the shoulder blade, just missing the collarbone. He undid his bandanna and, making a sort of tourniquet with it, wrapped it around Borg's upper arm. Taking another strip of cloth he first soaked it with water and then jammed it into the hole the bullet had made. Over it he fixed another piece of cloth and then finally he bound it all in place with a strip of rawhide.

'Best I can do,' Dwayne muttered. 'Leastways it might hold till we can get you to the doc. And on the way, you can tell me just what happened here.'

It was getting late and Brockley Whin realized he needed to find somewhere to set up camp for the night. The branding operation had carried on into the dusk but the fires were now extinguished. The herd was bedded down and the night herders were circling the bedground; he could see the dim glow of their cigarettes in the darkness. The peculiar animal smell of the cattle came to his nostrils but the whole scene was strangely hushed. Suddenly there was a swishing sound. His hand dropped to his gun but then he grinned. It was only an owl; he must be getting jumpy. He became aware that it was growing colder. With a last glance at the scene below, he tugged at the reins and turned the buckskin back in the direction of the notch in the hills through which he had ridden. The horse trod carefully. After a short time they came across a trail leading down through some trees. At the bottom was a narrow wash with some rocks and it seemed to Whin that it offered as good a place as any to settle down for the night. It was a sheltered spot; the rocks would serve to reflect the warmth of his camp-fire and it wasn't far from where he had watched the herd. Climbing from leather, he gave the horse a rub-down and fed it with some corn he carried behind the saddle. He also carried some basic supplies and when he had built a fire he put a pan of bacon and beans on to heat and filled a battered pot with water from the brook. He unrolled his groundsheet and blankets and then settled down to eat and to drink his coffee. When he had finished he took out the makings and built himself a smoke. All in all, he began to feel quite mellow. It was a type of situation he was well used to. When he had finished his cigarette he sat forward and added a few sticks to the fire. Then he lay back, resting his head on his saddle for a pillow, and dozed off.

He awoke with a start, knowing that something had disturbed him but not sure what it was. He reached for his rifle. Dawn was breaking and the air was clear and cool. He rolled to one side and was just getting to his feet when a shot rang out and a bullet thudded into the blankets where he had been lying. He flung himself into the shelter of a rock and brought the Winchester to his shoulder. Another shot rang out and then another but he had only a vague idea of where they were coming from or how many men were involved. Then he heard the snicker of a horse and, glancing up and along the wash, caught a glimpse of a rider just about to disappear into some trees. Taking instant aim, he squeezed off a shot and heard a splash as someone dropped from the saddle into the water. Firing rapidly, he sent a fusillade of shots echoing down the stream-bed. His fire was returned and bullets began to ricochet around the rocks but his position was a good one. There was a lull, and he figured whoever it was, they were not keen to give away their position. They must have been careless in the first place or he must have had some kind of sixth sense because they should have been able to creep up on him all the way.

His eyes swept the terrain, looking for signs of their presence but there was too much cover. The sun began to rise and it seemed they were settling into some kind of stalemate when suddenly he thought he glimpsed some movement among the bushes further along the stream-bank in the opposite direction from where he had detected the man on the horse. He was about to loose a shot but there was no further indication of anyone being there and he decided, after his burst of firing, to conserve the rest of his ammunition. He couldn't be sure that anyone was there. If he had seen movement, it might have been nothing more than a bird or a leaf fluttering in the air.

Before he had time to think about it further, there was a fresh burst of fire from among the bushes in the opposite direction. Instinctively, he ducked as shards of stone flew up from the rocks. Before he had time to re-position himself he heard sounds from behind him and looked round to see a man standing over him with his rifle raised. Even in that moment he cursed himself for having relaxed his guard. He had been right about that movement among the bushes and he had been confounded by the sudden burst of covering fire.

'Throw the rifle to one side!' the man barked.

Whin instantly considered the possibility of swinging his rifle round in order to get in a shot but he realized that the man had the drop on him. He had no option but to do as he commanded.

'Now the six-guns!' the man said.

Whin unfastened his gun-belt and threw it next to the Winchester. As he did so he heard the sound of approaching footsteps and three other men appeared, coming from different directions.

'I got him,' the first man shouted.

Whin looked closely at him. He didn't easily forget a face, even one glimpsed only fleetingly. Besides, the man was wearing quite a distinctive red shirt. Whin had a feeling that this was one of the men who had attacked Jeb and the girl, the same ones he had seen and heard at the Forked Lightning. He realized he had been careless; he should never have allowed himself to get into this situation.

The three other men came up and two of them seized him and pinioned his arms.

'He shot Magruder,' one of them said.

Where's Johnny?' the first man said. 'I figure we let him decide what we do with the varmint.'

Ignoring him, the other man stepped forward and, swinging the butt of his rifle, brought it crashing into Whin's chin, splitting it open in a wide gash which spurted blood. Whin felt his senses reeling but struggled not to lose control. What happened next he wasn't quite sure. He heard an explosion and the man with the gun went spinning backwards. The other two released his arms and then, as he toppled forward, he heard another crash and one of them fell. The fourth man had his gun in his hand; it was belching flame and smoke. He was sufficiently aware to know that he must do something to stop him so he flung out his foot, catching the man's leg behind the knee so that he fell backwards. The man landed heavily on top of him as a blackness descended and he remembered no more.

When he came to he was lying on the ground and someone was sitting nearby. His chin hurt and he felt confused. As his senses returned his first reaction was that the man must be one of his attackers but as he struggled to sit upright, the man got to his feet and approached him. He had a feeling that he recognized him from somewhere. The man was carrying a flask and when he bent down to hand it to him, he suddenly realized it was Underwood.

'How are you feelin'?' Underwood said. 'Take a swig of this; it should help.'

Whin took the flask and drank. In a moment he was spluttering and wiping his mouth with the back of his hand.

'Brandy,' Underwood said. 'It'll do you good.'

'Ain't like any brandy I ever tasted before,' Whin replied.

'Forty-rod with grape juice. It comes to the same thing.'

Whin took another swig. Having survived the first shock, he began to feel better.

'Underwood,' he said. 'Hell, what are you doin' here? You're just about the last person I'd expect to see.'

'Good job I decided to follow you,' Underwood said. 'If I hadn't found your sign, I figure you'd be dead by now. Those gentlemen looked like they meant business.'

'What happened?'

'Looked to me like they was fixin' themselves a necktie party with you in the main role. You did good to kick that varmint's feet from under him, though, or neither of us might be here now.'

Whin got to his feet. His horse was standing nearby and his gun-belt lay on the ground. He picked it up and fastened it round his waist.

'The rifle's back in its scabbard,' Underwood remarked.

'What happened to the gunnies?' Whin asked.

'The ones who had you – what's left of them – are over behind those bushes. The one you shot is down the river apiece. There was another one, but he got away. I guess you'd better tell me what's been happenin'. I assume those varmints are some of Tasker's boys.'

Whin bent his knees and then began to stretch. His chin was raw and painful but he was OK. Quickly, he outlined what had occurred at the Forked Lightning and his subsequent departure. When he got to the part where he had found the herd, he really had Underwood's attention.

'So we were right about Tasker having some place to hide away all the critters he and his boys have been rustlin',' he snapped.

'Yeah. I figure the whole herd, Tasker's and whatever other stock he's acquired, are all gathered in that one spot and I reckon they're ready for the trail. If that's the case, I got a little plan to hold 'em up.'

Underwood grinned. He didn't need to have things spelled out. 'You thinkin' of settin' off a little stampede?' he said.

Whin nodded. 'The only thing I'm a bit worried about is whether any of Tasker's boys might have heard the shootin',' he said, 'but I don't think it's likely. We're a good way from the bedding ground and the hills would have muffled the sound.'

Underwood's eyes looked up at the trail winding down from the higher ground. 'What are we waitin' for?' he said. He began to move towards his horse but hesitated when he looked at Whin again. 'You took a big blow to the chin,' he said. 'That's a nasty wound. If you want to wait a while—'

Whin's expression was steely. 'No waitin',' he replied. 'It's time Tasker started payin' his dues.'

They swung into leather but before they started up

the trail, Whin held out his hand for Underwood to take. 'Thanks,' he said. 'I owe you.'

Back in Blackwater, Willow Giroux had had no chance to raise the question of her marriage with Jeb Crossan since he had spoken with her by the banks of Blackwater Lake. Her father's time had been fully occupied with looking after the general store and since her mother's decline her own time had been largely taken up by household duties. On the afternoon of the day that Marshal Dwayne paid a visit to the Circle C, however, she was surprised to see her father coming up the path through the garden. She ran out to meet him.

'You're back early,' she said.

'Yes. Things were slack so I decided to close up.' She took his arm and they walked together up the porch steps and into the front room.

'How's your mother?' he said.

'The last time I looked in, she was asleep.' Looking closely at him, she realized how tired and drawn he looked. 'You sit down. I'll make some coffee,' she said.

She went into the kitchen and while she was making the coffee she heard his footsteps on the stairs and then the sound of the bedroom door being gently opened. She paused to listen and after a few moments she heard voices talking softly. So her mother was awake. She carried on making the coffee and then carried it through. By the time she had poured two mugs her father reappeared.

'Is Mother OK?' she asked.

He nodded and made to sit down but then straightened up again. 'Say,' he remarked, 'would you like to come for a walk?'

She looked at him in surprise. 'What about the coffee?' she said.

He glanced from her to the table where the coffee pot and the cups stood, seemingly slightly disoriented. 'Oh yes,' he murmured. 'The coffee.'

She looked at him and smiled. 'I'd like that,' she said, going back to what he had just said. 'I can make some more when we come back.'

As they made for the door there was a call from upstairs. 'Wait a moment,' Giroux said. 'I'll be right back.'

He ran up the stairs and into the bedroom where his wife was lying. Willow, standing at the foot of the stairs, heard the murmur of voices and then her father came back down.

'Is she OK?' Willow asked.

'Sure. She was just askin' why I was back so early.'

It seemed to Willow that the question was one her mother would more likely have asked the first time her father had called in to see her, but she didn't say anything. Together, she and her father started down the path she had last walked with Jeb and that made her think of what they had discussed. Now seemed as good a time as any to broach the subject of her marriage with her father but she didn't say anything for the moment.

They walked down the path to the lake in silence but when they came out on the lakeside her father seemed to become more animated.

'Look,' he said.

'Look at what?' she replied.

'I don't know. Just look.'

His gaze swept the whole circumference of the lake and then came to rest on her face.

'You know, I ain't taken near enough time just to enjoy a view like this,' he said. 'I haven't really appreciated it.'

'It's beautiful,' she replied.

He took her by the arm. 'Come on,' he said, 'let's walk on a little further.'

They walked round the edge of the lake past the jetty till they came to a break in the trees. It seemed dark by contrast with the open sunlight but it wasn't long till the trees thinned and they came to an open space.

'Me and your mother used to walk through here once,' he said, strolling forward.

Willow came up to him. 'Mother wasn't always. . . .' she began but stopped because she wasn't sure what she meant to say. Before she could continue, he spoke again.

'You and Jeb', he said. 'You remind me. . . .' He didn't seem able to complete what he had meant to say either and for a few moments they stood in silence, slightly leaning together. She was about to reply when he spoke again.

'Jeb's a fine young man,' he said. 'I like him a lot. You seem good together.' He moved slightly to one side and then turned to her and put his arm around her. 'If I'm right, and you feel the way about each other that I think you do, I'd say don't let any time go by. Don't let anything . . . I'm not expressing myself very well. Guess I must be gettin' old or somethin'.'

Willow put her head on his shoulder. 'Jeb and I, we were thinkin',' she began but before she could complete the sentence he gently placed a finger upon her lips.

'Get married,' he said. 'If you feel that way, if that's what you want, get married.' He looked down at her and smiled. 'Get married, but don't forget your old man.'

CHAPTER FIVE

Whin and Underwood crouched behind some boulders, looking down on the herd, which had been bedded down for the night. Earlier that day Whin had led the way along the trail leading back to the vantage point from which he had viewed Tasker's men at their business. When they got there, a different scene had met their eyes. The cattle had gone, but it was easy to see their trail and a cloud of dust in the distance. Spurring their horses, they had set off in pursuit until eventually they had got ahead of the herd and finally taken up their position overlooking the bedground.

Slowly the hours passed, the silence broken from time to time by the stamp of a horse or the cough of a shifting cow. The camp-fires of the cowboys had faded and the only lights to be seen were the dull glow of the lantern on the tongue of the chuck wagon or the faint, flickering point of a lighted cigarette. Off in the distance there came the occasional hoot of an owl.

'What are we waitin' for?' Underwood breathed.

'The graveyard stretch is just comin' to an end,' Whin replied. 'When they change the watch we'll move in.'

They observed closely the looming shapes of the night-herders. Occasionally the black mass of a cow would move out from the shadows and one of the riders would swing towards it, easing it back into the sleeping herd. Presently two more riders appeared, coming from the direction of the remuda.

'OK,' Whin whispered. 'Looks like the relief men have arrived.'

The new guard approached the two men who had been circling the herd and after a few moments the off-herd riders started to move in the direction of the chuck wagon. Whin and Underwood were already on their feet. They stepped into leather and began to urge their horses down the long slope that led to the bench on which the cattle had been settled. When they were part of the way down they drew their sixguns.

'Once those cows have skittered, remember to hightail it quick outta here,' Whin admonished.

They dug their spurs into their horses' flanks and began to move at a canter. As they gathered speed Whin raised his gun into the air and squeezed the trigger. The silence of the night was shattered as a salvo of shots from his gun and Underwood's boomed out, and in an instant the whole peaceful scene was transformed. People began to yell; there was a crashing of answering gunshots and the cattle came to their feet uttering loud bawls of terror. Whin and Underwood began to whoop, adding to the confusion. Tasker's men came running and tumbling from where they had been lying, taking up their guns and firing blindly into the darkness and for a few moments the night was a scene of pandemonium. With a growing thunder of hoofs, the longhorns began to run. Some of the older cowhands, sizing up the situation, began to shout to the men to get after the stampeding cattle. At the same time Whin became aware that a group of riders was moving up the slope towards them.

'They've seen us!' he yelled.

They were towards the bottom of the slope and Whin intended riding his horse parallel to the line of the ridge, but too late he saw that some of the cows had turned and he was in danger of becoming embroiled in the stampede. He tried to warn Underwood but Underwood wasn't where he expected him to be. The dark mass of the main body of the herd was charging across the prairie with a noise like a steam train and the group, which had split, was coming at him fast. He was soon riding at breakneck speed to try and keep ahead of the herd but he didn't seem to be making ground. It was becoming hard to see what was happening because of the dust but the night was still rent by stabs of flame and he knew he was under fire. He was sur-rounded by glinting, tossing horns and the only thing he could do was run with the cattle. He was looking for a gap. If he could edge away he might make good his escape. He had no idea what had become of Underwood. All he knew was that things hadn't gone quite to plan. The gap he was looking for suddenly appeared and he put the horse over. He was worried that the buckskin might lose its footing. If it did, he would be trampled to death. The mass of longhorns, however, was thinning. He knew it wasn't the main herd. He could still hear the thunder of their hoofs but they were gone into the night. He edged through another gap and found himself on the periphery of the herd. He began to slow the horse down. There was room now for the maddened cattle to go past him and after another three-quarters of a mile he was free of the press of cattle. He slowed the horse further, looking about him for signs of pursuit, but he seemed to have shaken off Tasker's gunnies as well as his cows. He listened carefully for any sounds of approaching riders but couldn't detect any. The only sound was the diminishing pounding of hoofs. As he peered through the darkness, his eyes picked out a few shapes of scattered cattle.

There was no sign, however, of Underwood. Had he managed to avoid the stampeding longhorns? Whin determined to go back the way he had come, but rode first to the top of the ridge and down the other side. He started to retrace his steps. After a time he rode to the crest of the ridge again in order to get his bearings. No sooner had he done so than a shot rang out and he heard the whine of a bullet. He realized that dawn was coming up and he had sky-lined himself sufficiently for someone to take a pot-shot. He went over the crest again and began to ride towards a stand of cottonwoods. He rode into the trees and pulled up. Over the top of the ridge a rider appeared. He began to move down the slope towards him and as he got nearer he recognized the rider as Underwood. As he sat his horse, he couldn't help a wry grin from spreading across his features. What an irony it would have been if Underwood had rescued him from the gunslicks only to do their dirty work himself.

'Underwood, it's me, Whin!' he shouted. 'I'm comin' out from the trees.'

He rode forward. Underwood had drawn his horse to a halt but when he realized it was Whin he spurred it on.

'You damn fool, you coulda shot me!' Whin shouted. He came alongside and they leaned over to embrace one another.

'Hell!' Underwood said. 'I thought you were one of Tasker's gunnies. I figured it was either him or me. I figured you'd probably been trampled to death.'

Whin looked about him. The sun was coming up, beginning to diffuse light across the hills and valleys. 'You weren't far wrong,' he replied.

Underwood's face was suddenly wreathed in a smile. 'Goldurn it,' he said, 'we sure succeeded in scattering those longhorns. They're probably still runnin'. It ain't much, but it sure feels good to have done somethin' to hit back at Tasker.'

'Yeah. But I figure we need to get back to the Circle C. This is just a sideshow. From what we know, Tasker ain't goin' to lose any time now in carryin' out his plans. We're gonna be needed at the ranch.'

Together, they began to work their way down the trail.

Marshal Dwayne didn't take Borg all the way back to Blackwater. The man was badly hurt and it made more sense to leave him at the Circle C and send for the doctor. Crossan instructed one of his men to that effect.

'Better tell the undertaker to get out to the Stamp Iron sometime soon too,' Dwayne said without elaborating. Borg's story was soon told and confirmed everything that the marshal had been discussing earlier with Crossan and Dunlop.

When eventually Dwayne got back to Blackwater it was getting late and he was hungry. He made his way to the Black Cat dining parlour. Etta was back in the kitchen but quickly appeared as the door shut behind him.

'Marshal Dwayne,' she said. 'Just the man I wanted to see!'

'Why? Has something happened?'

She came over to his table and sat down. 'Some men came in earlier this afternoon,' she said. 'I didn't like them.'

'Why? What did they do?'

'They were . . . they started to make comments. It started like they were just joshing but it took a turn . . . it was unpleasant.'

'They didn't cause any actual trouble?'

'No, but I figure they would have if I'd have given them time. I asked them to leave.'

'And they did?'

'That's the funny part. Just at that point your deputy, Lugg, came in. They seemed to know him. He sat down with them and they began to calm down. I thought about telling him what had happened but it didn't seem as though he would be likely to do anything. After a time they all got up and left together.'

'So Lugg managed to handle the situation?'

'I guess it might sound that way, but it wasn't really like that. I got the feeling, almost, that Lugg was one of them. Like I say, they all left together. They didn't go because Lugg was forcin' them to behave.'

Dwayne scratched his chin, thinking about what Etta had just said, when she interrupted his thoughts.

'Anyway, that's not the point. I figure I got enough about me to handle a situation like that myself. That's not why I'm telling you this. No, I'm telling you because I'm sure I heard your name mentioned. Maybe I'm making something out of nothing, but I don't figure those men were up to any good. In fact, I'm sure they weren't. So I guess I'm just trying to warn you. I'm telling you, I had a real bad feeling about those *hombres*. And why would Lugg have anything to do with them? Because I'm sure he does.'

The marshal considered whether to mention any of his own suspicions about Lugg but decided that for the moment it might be better to keep them to himself.

'Thanks, Etta,' he said. 'I sure appreciate you tellin' me this. It certainly sounds as though there might be more to it than meets the eye. You didn't see where they all went to after leavin' the café?'

'They set off in the direction of the Diamondback. I figure they wanted something a bit stronger than coffee. Can't think why they would come in here in the first place.'

Dwayne ordered a plate of steak and hash. As he waited for it to arrive, he was thinking that the Black Cat might make as good a rendezvous as any if Lugg had arranged to meet with the rowdies. If so, what was he up to?

Whin and Underwood rode hard till they figured they were well clear of Tasker's hardcases. Once they were clear of the immediate vicinity, they felt that they were pretty safe because most of Tasker's men would be fully occupied trying to round up the herd. The fact that Whin had become embroiled with one group of longhorns they regarded as a good sign. A stampeding herd sometimes split into two or more sections which often ran in parallel. At other times it might scatter, making it all the more difficult to get the cattle together again.

'With any luck that's what happened,' Whin said.

'Either way those cows are gonna be spoiled,' Underwood replied. 'They'll be hard to hold now. They'll probably stampede again before they get much further.'

Whin was satisfied with what they had achieved, but, as he had said to Underwood, he realized it was only a sideshow. The majority of Tasker's gunnies had remained behind at the Forked Lightning and they were probably already on their way to carry out their assault on the small ranchers.

'How about we take a detour and see if we can find out what's happenin' there?' Underwood suggested.

Whin had considered the matter but it seemed to him that little would be gained by doing so and they would be taking an unnecessary risk. 'I figure we'd probably do better to get on back to the Circle C,' he replied.

Underwood nodded. 'It was just a thought,' he said. 'I think you're probably right.'

Shortly after noon they stopped to give their horses a break. They stretched out on the grass and rolled a couple of cigarettes. Whin's chin was causing him some pain but the tobacco seemed to soothe it. They smoked in silence, glad of the opportunity to rest after all the excitement. Underwood eventually changed his position so that he was leaning on one elbow and looking at his companion.

'Whin,' he said. 'You ain't said a lot about how you and Tasker got to know each other. I hope you don't mind me bringin' it up but I been thinkin' some and it seems to me there's got to be more to it than you've been lettin' on.'

Whin drew deeply on his cigarette and then turned to Underwood. 'You're right,' he said. 'There was somethin' more to it.' He stopped.

Underwood suddenly felt that maybe he had done the wrong thing in bringing the subject up. 'Sorry,' he said. 'It ain't any of my business.'

'No need to be sorry,' Whin replied. 'Besides, after everything that's happened, I figure it is your business. It might not have been before, but it is now.' He paused again, this time to build himself another smoke. He passed the tobacco pouch to Underwood who did the same.

'It was like this,' he continued. 'I think I told you that me and Tasker once rode for the same outfit up in the Panhandle. One time we had to trail a herd up to Baxter Springs. Were you ever there?'

Underwood shook his head.

'Man, it was pretty rough. The place only lasted for one summer, but durin' that time I reckon she musta been the liveliest place in the West. Not that we saw too much of the place because we found ourselves facing a barrier of armed farmers. They weren't too pleased about havin' us cowpunchers around and they were supported by a whole bunch of jayhawkers. Hell, I guess that's beside the point except it was Tasker who saved me from gettin' lynched by a bunch of the varmints. I'd ridden off alone and they bushwhacked me. For a time it looked like my number was up till Tasker turned up with a few of the other boys from the outfit.'

'Kind of ironic,' Underwood said, 'considerin' what some of Tasker's own boys tried to do to you.'

Something clicked in Whin's memory. The gunnie who had crept up on him and surprised him had referred to another one named Johnny. What was it Tasker had told him? That Baltimore Johnny was one of his main gunhawks? Maybe Baltimore Johnny was the one who, according to Underwood, had got away.

'I figure an *hombre* by name of Baltimore Johnny might have had more to do with that than Tasker,' Whin replied. 'At least, I'm hopin' so.'

'Baltimore Johnny?'

'He's one of Tasker's gunslicks. You won't have heard of him, but I've come across the name before. Even ran across him once. Seems like he made a reputation for himself back east before things got too hot and he had to light out.'

'So what happened to Tasker? From what you say, it sounds like he was different then.'

Whin shrugged. 'I don't know. Maybe I had the wrong impression. On the other hand, people change, I guess. We went our different ways. Maybe it was bein' successful changed him.'

They sat quietly for a while, finishing their smokes. Then they got to their feet and stepped back into leather. Whin's eyes searched their backtrail but he could see no signs of pursuit. Touching their spurs to the horses' flanks, they rode on towards the Circle C.

When he had finished his meal, Marshal Dwayne stepped out into the street. Evening was closing in and there was an unusual stillness about the town. A few people remained on the streets; a lone horseman appeared from around a corner and rode up to the Diamondback saloon where he dismounted and tied his horse to the hitch-rail. He glanced towards the marshal before stepping through the batwing doors. Dwayne was just about to make his own way there when a buggy came rolling down the street with the doctor driving it. Dwayne stepped off the boardwalk as the buggy came to a halt. 'How's Borg?' he asked.

'He's taken a few knocks but he'll be OK,' the doctor replied. He looked up at Dwayne. 'What's goin' on?' he continued. 'There was quite a lot of activity around the Circle C. I got the impression that they were preparing for some kinda trouble.'

'You're right, Doc,' Dwayne replied. 'It seems like Tasker has had enough of trying to shift Crossan and Dunlop by more or less legal means. I fear he might be about to take matters into his own hands.'

'Is that why Borg got hurt?' Doc Smith said.

Dwayne nodded and, seeing there was no point in trying to conceal what had occurred at the Stamp Iron, he gave the doctor a brief outline of what he had found there.

'That's terrible,' the doctor replied. 'I never liked that ornery varmint Tasker. I guess I ain't the only one to have seen the way he's more or less taken over this town and I don't like it. Quite a lot of the other folk don't like it either. But this is somethin'

108

altogether more serious.'

The doctor's words gave Dwayne an idea. 'I'm still hopin' that we could be mistaken and the whole affair might come to nothin',' he said.

'A bit late for that,' Doc Smith interjected. 'Considerin' what you just told me.'

'Yeah, you're right.' The doctor's words brought home to Dwayne the gravity of the situation. It was as if the shock of coming across what he had found at the Stamp Iron had had a numbing effect, from which he was only now beginning to emerge. It made the thought that just then came into his mind even more relevant and urgent.

'Doc, I agree with you. I think a lot of the townspeople feel the way you've just described. Given that's the case, do you figure we could roust up some of 'em to help out if it's come to a fight?'

There was a steely look in the doctor's eye. 'You've got one volunteer already,' he replied. 'If you like, I could ask around. To be honest, I figure some folks won't need much persuadin'.'

'Still, that should be my job,' Dwayne replied. 'But, the way things are shapin' up, I figure I could do with some help. Yes, sure, I'd appreciate it. But be careful. We don't want to cause any sort of panic. Tasker's quarrel ain't with the town but with the ranchers.'

'The town's been drawn into it,' the doctor

replied. 'It's in our interest to do somethin' to stop Tasker as well as the ranchers. Leave it to me.'

'It's late now,' the marshal said.

'Not too late,' the doctor replied. 'I'll see what I can do. Come over to my place tomorrow early and we'll see what we've got.'

The doctor tugged at the reins and the buggy moved away down the street. Dwayne felt that something useful had been accomplished but he felt restless. He started off in the opposite direction to the Diamondback saloon; coming to a junction, he turned down the adjoining street. Night had fallen and a cool breeze blew up from the direction of Blackwater Lake, towards which he bent his steps. It did him good to be walking and by the time he came on the lake he was feeling better. It had been a hard day and he had been more affected by events than he realized. The water gave off a cool freshness and the wind blew in the treetops. He began to walk around the lake towards the jetty, beyond which lay the western edge of town where the Giroux property was located. As he looked in that direction, he saw a dark shape outlined against the shoreline. Instinctively his hand dropped to his holster but then something about the figure seemed familiar and he began instead to make his way towards it, taking care not to reveal himself. As he got closer he could see the figure was that of Giroux. He stepped clear of the trees and called out the storekeeper's name.

'Giroux, it's Marshal Dwayne!'

Giroux turned to face him as he stepped on the jetty and took a few paces along it. 'Dwayne,' he replied. 'Is that you?'

The marshal came alongside him. 'Didn't expect to see anyone out here,' he said.

'Felt like a breath of air,' Giroux responded. 'It's a pleasant evening.'

Clouds had blown up and the air was quite chill. It didn't seem to the marshal that the night was particularly propitious but he didn't disagree with Giroux.

'What about you, Marshal?' Giroux continued. 'Don't see you down here much apart from the fishin'. I take it you ain't here for that tonight.'

'I felt like a breath of air too.'

He looked out over the blackness of the lake. Underneath their feet the dark waters sucked at the piling of the jetty and an occasional splash suggested the presence of something alien and hidden.

'How's your wife?' he asked.

'Pretty much the same,' Giroux replied. 'Doc Smith was over again just yesterday but he don't seem able to tell what's wrong with her.'

They were both silent for a few moments. It seemed to the marshal that Giroux was reluctant to continue that line of conversation. When he spoke again it was about Jeb and Willow.

'They've decided to bring the wedding forward,' he said. 'They've already been over to see the Reverend and Etta Foy is happy to be handlin' the victuals.'

'That's good,' Dwayne replied. 'That's real good.' He realized how low he had been feeling recently and the storekeeper's words genuinely cheered him. At the same time he felt an inclination to take Giroux into his confidence and tell him about what he had seen at the Stamp Iron. It had been only earlier that same day but it seemed a long time ago.

'Jeb's a good boy but he'd better be careful. I wouldn't like to see anythin' happen to spoil things.'

'You're referrin' to the bushwhackin' affair?'

'That and other things.'

'It's funny, but the doc was sayin' somethin' similar when I spoke to him. There have been rumours goin' around town.' Giroux turned to face the marshal. 'Look, if things are comin' to a head with Tasker, count me in. You don't need to beat about the bush. It's pretty common knowledge that trouble is brewin' and that Tasker's the man responsible. I know it was some of his hired guns that did the dry-gulchin'. I owe it to Willow and Jeb to take my share doin' some-thin' about it. I may be only a shopkeeper, but I figure I can handle a gun. If it's finally come to a showdown, you can count me in.'

The marshal was about to respond by telling

112

Giroux in more detail what had transpired that day when his eye was caught by a glimmer among the trees by the path leading to the Girouxs' house. For a moment he thought it might be Willow or even Giroux's wife but then he realized how unlikely that would be. Before he had time for further thought there was a stab of flame and the boom of a rifle. A bullet whistled past his head; a moment later there was another report and a bullet thudded into the wooden post at the end of the jetty. Dwayne moved towards Giroux to drag him down but his foot slipped and before he could do anything to prevent it, he had tumbled into the cold murky waters of the lake.

He sank down. Instinctively his feet sought the bottom but they failed to find it. Panic began to seize him because he couldn't swim. He thrashed about, seeking the surface, but the weight of his clothes was pulling him down. All around him was blackness and then, somehow, his head broke through to the air and he gulped desperately, seeking to fill his bursting lungs. He heard loud bangs and saw flashes of light which he thought were inside his head till he realized that shooting was taking place. He looked up towards the jetty and fancied he could see the kneeling form of Giroux. The reverberation of a gun rang out; there was another flash and he understood that Giroux was involved in a firefight with some gunnies

113

further around the shore. He had a pretty shrewd idea who they were. Was Lugg one of them?

He felt himself being pulled under again and began to move his arms and legs in a desperate effort to keep afloat. It was a losing battle as his head dipped under the water again, but as he sank downward a kind of fury seemed to take possession of him. He wasn't going to be defeated. The situation was absurd. Although he had fallen off the end of the jetty, it didn't project more than ten feet into the lake. He was so close to safety. He wasn't going to allow Tasker's gunhawks to get the better of him or Giroux. He had a vision of the grisly scene that had met his eyes at the Stamp Iron. There was no way he was going to let Tasker get away with it. Jubal and Jeb Crossan, Dunlop, and now the doctor and Giroux, they were good people and they needed him. Gathering all his remaining strength and resolve, he forced himself to stay calm. He mustn't panic. That only made matters worse. Kicking his legs and pulling back his arms, he strove with all his might to rise up again and succeeded once more in breaking the surface. He turned over so that he was lying on his back and began to kick towards the shore. His head kept going under and his nostrils and ears were filled with water. He started to sink again, but when he put out his leg to try and arrest his descent, this time his foot was stopped by something solid. He lowered his other leg and found that he able to stand. The water was up to his chin but as he stumbled forward he rose slowly out of the water so it was up to his chest and then his thighs. As he struggled in the shallows, he fell and felt himself being dragged back into the water. Something seemed to be caught around his foot; despite his resolve he felt panic begin to surge up again but at the same time he became aware of a figure that had appeared on the shore and he heard a voice calling his name. The figure splashed into the water next to him.

'My foot!' he spluttered.

The person reached down and after a moment he felt the pressure on his foot relax.

'It was caught on some sort of snag,' a voice murmured. Dwayne felt an arm round his shoulders, assisting him the rest of the way to the shore. Together they clambered up the low bank where Dwayne finally lay, coughing and spluttering. When he had recovered a little, he looked up. It wasn't a man who had come to his rescue; it was Willow Giroux! Only now did he realize that the sound of gunfire had ceased.

'Your father,' he managed to gasp. 'He needs help.'

'My father's OK. I think my arrival scared off the bushwhackers.'

As if to back up what Willow had just said, they

heard the sound of running steps and Giroux himself appeared.

'Is the marshal OK?' he gasped.

Dwayne had struggled to his knees and now he managed to stand up. 'Sure, I'm OK,' he sputtered. 'Leastways, I will be in a few minutes.'

Giroux turned to his daughter. 'We'll get him back to the house. I figure that whoever was waitin' to take a pot-shot at us has gone but we'll need to be careful.'

'We could circle round through the trees. It might be safer.'

Giroux suddenly looked anxious. 'What about your mother?' he said. 'She's alone now in the house.'

'It was me those varmints were interested in,' Dwayne managed to say. 'I don't think there's any reason to think anyone else might be in any danger.'

'All the same, we'd better get back quick,' Giroux replied. 'Are you up to makin' a move, Marshal?'

'Sure, I'm fine. Let's get goin'.'

'You lead the way, Willow,' her father said. 'But keep a lookout.'

They started back through the trees. It was dark but Willow seemed to know the way and it didn't take them long to reach the Giroux property. Giroux ran ahead into the house and as Willow and Dwayne entered he re-appeared. His face was drawn and ashen but relief was written across it.

116

'She's still asleep,' he said.

Willow took control of the situation. 'Sit down, Father,' she said. 'I'll find Mr Dwayne some dry clothes and then make us some coffee.'

Dwayne turned to her. 'I ain't had a chance to say a proper thank-you,' he said. 'I figure I owe it to you for gettin' me out of that water.'

'It was nothing. You had already almost reached the shore.'

'All the same, I don't know if I'd have made it if you hadn't been there.'

'It was just lucky I happened to come by.'

'What were you doing there?' Giroux asked.

She smiled. 'I saw you go out. I had a feeling you might be down by the lake. I just thought I'd join you.'

'Did you see anything as you made your way from the house?' Dwayne asked.

'No. I didn't notice anything at all till the shooting started,' Willow replied.

'What do you make of it?' Giroux said.

'Etta Foy was tellin' me about a bunch of no-goods who were in her eating house earlier. She warned me about them. I figure they were responsible for this.' He was going to mention his suspicions about Lugg but decided to leave that out for the moment.

'Let me get you those dry clothes,' Willow interposed. She went out of the room and Giroux looked at the marshal.

'There's a connection between those varmints and what happened here and what happened with Willow and Jeb Crossan, isn't there?' he said.

The marshal nodded.

'I got a personal stake in dealin' with the scum,' Giroux said. 'Whatever steps you might be intendin' to take, I'm here to back you up.'

Willow could be heard moving about upstairs.

'That's quite a girl you got there,' the marshal said. 'Jeb Crossan is sure a lucky boy.'

He looked back at Giroux. 'Appreciate what you just said. But there are a few other things I think you need to know.'

Giroux uttered a low grunt. 'Well, once you get those dry clothes on we can sit and talk. And I figure we could both do with something a mite stronger to drink to back up Willow's coffee.'

CHAPTER SIX

Tasker stood on the veranda of his ranch house and surveyed the mass of riders gathered in the yard. It was still dark but they were as mean-looking a bunch of hardcases as he had come across and they were all eager for action. They had been cooped up around the Forked Lightning for too long. The time had come to let them loose on the Circle C, the Box W and anyone else who might still be prepared to offer any resistance to him. So far this whole affair had been a calculated business but now an extra dimension had been added and Tasker found himself as keen to set about putting the ranchers in their place as his gang of desperados.

It had taken him some time to calm down following the disappearance of Brockley Whin, which had only served to confirm what his men had told him about Whin's interference on behalf of the Crossan boy and his girlfriend. He had gone out of his way to give Whin a chance and he felt as though he had been betrayed. Then Baltimore Johnny had returned with the news of the latest incident involving Whin. He wasn't sure just what Whin's game was, but since Whin had departed in the direction of where the herd was gathered, it couldn't be anything to his advantage. The only thing he knew for certain was that Whin had opted to side with the small ranchers. At some point he would catch up with his former friend and then he would deal with him in the way he deserved. He could hardly wait for that time to come. He looked round once more, then strode down from the veranda and stepped into leather.

'OK, boys!' he shouted. 'I figure the time's come to deal with those stinkin' nesters once and for all.'

At his words the gunnies began to yell and cheer and a few took out their six-guns and began firing into the air. Tasker turned to Baltimore Johnny.

'What you boys did at the Stamp Iron is gonna be child's play compared with what's gonna happen to those nesters now,' he sneered.

A wolfish grin spread across the gunman's face. 'The boys have been waitin' for this,' he said. 'That other thing just kinda whetted their appetite.'

'They'll have plenty to feed on,' Tasker replied. He raised himself in the stirrups and yelled loudly to make himself heard above the din.

'OK, men! Let's go get 'em!'

With a loud rattle and clatter of hoofs, the band of gunslicks rode out of the dusky yard in a cloud of dust.

Back at the Circle C, the time following the return of Whin and Underwood had been passed in a strange atmosphere of unreality. Jubal Crossan had put the place at the disposal of the people who had come together to face up to Tasker and his gun-toting band of outlaws, and they comprised an oddly sorted crew. In addition to Jubal, Jeb, Underwood and Whin, the doctor was there with five of the townsfolk he had brought along with him. Borg had wanted to come but the doc had insisted he stay behind and arranged for Etta Foy to look in on him. The doc had also taken time to see to Whin's damaged chin. Giroux had left Willow in charge of the store while he was away. He had not told his daughter all the details about what was happening, but she did not need to have it spelled out. She was doubly anxious, for her father and for Jeb, but she had put a brave face on it. Finally, Dunlop from the Box W had come over, accompanied by Chet Hoover, his range boss, and some of his cowhands. He had left the rest of them to keep an eye on the ranch. Everyone felt certain that Tasker's main objective would be the Circle C and preparations had already begun for the defence of the place when Whin, who had been thinking hard about the matter, suggested a possible alternative.

'Fighting a defensive battle here at the Circle C makes a lot of sense,' he said, 'but it also means we could get bottled up. Tasker could even play a waiting game and either starve us out or pick us off at his convenience.'

'We've got plenty of supplies,' Crossan replied. 'We could hold out for a long time.'

'Yeah, but I'm thinkin' it might be a better idea for us to take the battle to him. All along he's held the initiative. Maybe it's about time we figured on givin' him a surprise.'

'Like we did with the stampede,' Underwood said. 'Hell, he wouldn't have been expectin' that.'

'I think maybe Whin's got a point,' Dunlop interjected.

'Have you got somethin' in mind?' Hoover said. 'And by the way, Whin, I don't think I've apologized yet for suspectin' you of killin' Glanton.'

'No hard feelin's,' Whin replied. 'You did the right thing. I guess it sure looked that way.' He paused and then turned back to Crossan.

'I've taken some note of the lie of the land,' he said, 'but you obviously know the terrain better than me. I'm wonderin' if we could catch Tasker off-guard and spring a surprise attack on him someplace just where he'd be likely to hit Circle C territory. Takin' into account the fact that we can't be entirely certain which way he'll come, can you think of somewhere on his likely route that might fit the bill?'

Jubal's brows creased in thought. Presently his features lightened. 'Sure,' he said. He turned to Jeb. 'They're most likely to have to come through the north-east range. There's some pretty rough country out that way, the sort of place some of the old mossy-horns like to hide in. There's quite a bit of timber too. If it's an ambush you've got in mind, that place could offer possibilities.' At his father's words Jeb became animated.

'Pa's right,' he said. 'I ain't been out that way recently because it's pretty much at the limit of decent cattle range, but I remember there's an old line shack that ain't been used in a long time. It'll be in a bad state but it's right next to the trail and we could maybe make use of it.'

'Good thinkin',' Dunlop said. 'I think we could be on to somethin' here. It seems to be a better idea to take the fight to Tasker and meet with him out in the open than sit and wait here, twiddlin' our thumbs.'

'Yes,' Whin said, 'but we don't need to expose ourselves unduly. It might come to an open fire fight in the end, but if we use our heads and take advantage of the terrain, we might be able to pick off some of Tasker's gunnies before it ever comes to that. Leastways it might serve to even up the odds a little.'

'Makes sense to me,' Hoover replied. 'Reminds me of the tactics we sometimes used in the war. Why don't we head out that way and get ready for Tasker?' There was a murmur of agreement.

'Let's just hope Tasker does what we expect him to do,' the doc added.

Tasker hadn't led his gang of gunslicks very far when a group of riders appeared out of the darkness riding towards them. He held up his hand and his group came to a halt.

'Looks like folks don't care about their health,' Baltimore Johnny commented.

Tasker peered closely. 'It's Lugg,' he said, 'with a few of the others.' The riders drew closer and finally came to a halt.

'Well?' Tasker said. 'What happened this time?'

'We got him,' Lugg replied. 'This time he didn't get away.'

'You're quite sure of that? You might find it difficult to become town marshal if Dwayne is still around.'

'Me and the boys caught up with him right by the lake last night,' Lugg replied. 'I saw him fall in. I figure he took a bullet first. Either way, he's dead.'

Tasker nodded. 'OK,' he said. 'Good work. Now fall in with the rest of them.'

Lugg glanced around. 'We're on our way, then?' he said.

'We sure are,' Tasker replied.

The little party of riders, led by Jubal Crossan, rode away from the Circle C ranch house and started towards the north-east range. During the course of the first hour Whin reckoned to have seen some sixty head of cattle, looking sleek and ready for the round-up.

'How many head of cattle do you and your father run?' he asked Jeb.

'Three hundred,' he replied. 'A few less, thanks to Tasker and his rustlin' varmints.'

'When this is over,' Whin said, 'I'd be happy to lend a hand gettin' them up the trail.'

Jeb grinned. 'Sure thing,' he replied.

After a time the nature of the country began to change, becoming rougher and more broken with patches of mesquite and dry watercourses. There were few signs of cattle now – just a sprinkling of them – so it came as something of a surprise to Whin when they came on a cabin of quite a substantial size with a tumbledown stables and a pole corral nearby. It had clearly not been used in some time. Jubal Crossan brought the little troupe of riders to a halt.

'This is the place I think Jeb had in mind. Is that right, son?' he said.

'Yeah, I think this is it. There might be others but as you can see, the trail comes by quite close. I figure if we put some men in there, we could give Tasker and his boys a hot reception.'

Whin's eyes swept the local terrain. 'There's quite a bit of cover,' he said. 'I reckon we could put some men in that big grove of trees over yonder. Then we can draw Tasker in here and hit him from behind when he ain't expectin' it. That way he'll be fightin' on two fronts, as it were.'

'Good idea,' Jubal confirmed. 'And what's more, he won't know how many of us he has to contend with. 'Specially if we position ourselves right. We can make it look like we got a lot more men than we have.'

'I think this is the spot where we make our stand,' Dwayne said. 'Like the doc said earlier, now all we got to do is hope we're right about Tasker and that he comes this way.'

The others grinned. 'We're gonna look kinda of foolish holed up here if he don't,' Dunlop said.

By the time they had taken up their posts, the daylight was beginning to fade. Dusk became darkness and thickened into black night. There was no way of telling when Tasker might appear. Whin felt it was unlikely to be during the night but he couldn't be certain. As the hours ticked by and it seemed less and less likely that he would show, they set up a guard duty rota; while two men watched the trail, the rest of them

gathered in the line shack to take some rest. A couple
of hours after midnight, Whin and Underwood took
up their positions on either side of the trail. Whin had
been trying to recall what Tasker had said to him
about his plans but from what he could remember, the
timings had been uncertain. Tasker had said something about maybe riding out in two or three days'
time. It was his growing conviction that the next day
would be the likeliest. He settled down to watch, his
back resting against the trunk of a tree. Underwood
had taken up a position further back towards the line
cabin, which loomed black and somehow threatening
further off against the night sky. Whin could have
done with a smoke but didn't build one because he
knew, as they all did, that they could not risk giving
away their position. His senses were always alert, but
he found himself suddenly thinking about Etta Foy
back at the Black Cat dining parlour in town.
Blackwater seemed a decent place. It was a shame that
Tasker was gradually taking it over. He felt that it
wasn't just for the sake of the small ranchers that he
was waiting here, not knowing whether tomorrow or
the next day he was to live or die.

Whin was right about it being unlikely that Tasker
would make his approach during the night. When
dawn broke, they all made a quick breakfast at the
line cabin before returning to their places. Whin
resumed the position he had taken during the night

127

but Giroux took the place of Underwood. Placed at strategic points in the vicinity of the cabin were Dunlop and his men from the Box W together with the marshal, some of the townsfolk and Underwood, while in the line cabin itself were the Crossans together with some men from the Circle C. The doctor and the rest of the townsmen had taken up positions in the stables next to the corral, where their horses were all concealed.

The light grew, draping pearly mist over the landscape. Whin, who had been watching the trail, turned his head in the direction of the corral. There was a hollow behind the line cabin where the mist gathered, and for a few moments he could see nothing. Then, on the fringes of the mist, he thought he saw something move, something shadowy and vague. He thought at first that it was just an effect of the shifting vapour and then he perceived figures, faint and ghostly, moving to and fro. Even then he failed to grasp their significance, thinking that they must be Circle C hands carrying out some last-minute defensive work. Then there came the sudden bark of a rifle and the realization that they were not Circle C men, but some of Tasker's gunnies.

He didn't stop to ask himself how they had got there. There was no need now for him to give the prearranged signal because gunfire suddenly began to erupt from the line cabin. He raised his

Winchester, drew a bead on the nearest figure in the corral, and squeezed the trigger, even though he realized that the man was probably out of range. Guns were barking from the cover of the brush where the rest of the men were hidden but as far as Whin could tell it wasn't having a lot of effect. The shadowy figures in the corral had disappeared and Whin assumed they must have taken cover when, from the stables, there arose a clatter of noise and from both the back and front of the building horses began to plunge in a terrified gallop.

'They've spooked the horses!' Whin shouted.

He had no idea what had happened there, whether the doc and the townsfolk had been caught unprepared or had managed to respond to the assault. He got to his feet and was about to run towards the line cabin when he halted in his tracks. Coming from somewhere back along the trail he heard the distant rumble of horses. He ducked down again and turned in that direction. There was no mistaking the sound now. It could only be Tasker approaching with his main body of gunslicks. The men who had loosed the horses must have been an advance party. Had they come upon the line cabin by chance or had it been a deliberate assault? His guess was that they had spotted something suspicious about the cabin. He hadn't heard the sound of their horses. It didn't matter now. The main battle was about to commence.

If the sounds of struggle and mayhem at the line cabin had reached Tasker's ears, it didn't seem to affect his approach. There was no attempt at restraint on the part of the gunnies; they just came riding in regardless. Whin guessed that Tasker was underestimating the strength of the opposition; if that was the case, it could only be to the ranchers' advantage. As they got closer, the gunnies' attention seemed to be on what was happening at the line cabin. The consequence was that they were even more unprepared for the fusillade of fire which hit them as they got close. When the smoke cleared a little, Whin saw that a number of horses and riders were down. The rest had halted but soon they began to scatter, firing wildly as they rode.

Whin had rapidly reloaded after the first salvo and now loosed off a further volley. Stabs of flame were coming from the brush all around where Giroux and the others were placed; when he glanced along the line of fire, he had a glimpse of Marshal Dwayne as he pumped away at the mass of riders. He couldn't see what was happening at the line cabin but he assumed Jubal Crossan and his men were dealing with the gunnies there and in the outbuildings. It had been a good idea to station the doctor with some men in the stables, but had they been alert to the danger? Above the rattle of gunfire he could hear the whinnying of horses but it was impossible to tell whether they were the gunslicks' mounts or their own.

The scene was one of total confusion. Whin had no way of knowing what was happening at the line cabin; whether Tasker and his gang had been taken by surprise or were on top in the battle. Bullets were raining all around him and from their trajectories he figured that most of them were coming from the trees and bushes along the trail. That could only mean that Tasker's men, or a good number of them, had found shelter there. What about Tasker himself? He had been trying to catch sight of him when the gunnies had first appeared in sight, but he had not been able to pick him out.

If Whin had not been able to see Tasker, Marshal Dwayne had been more fortunate in picking out the unmistakable figure of Lugg, and he was pretty sure that Lugg had seen him. For a moment their eyes had met as Lugg wheeled his horse away before dropping from the saddle to seek shelter in the bushes. Dwayne wasn't surprised to see Lugg in the enemy's vanguard; after all, it only confirmed what he already knew. But when he saw him riding along with the rest of the gunnies, a kind of fury seized him. That man had betrayed and double-crossed him. He had posed as an agent of the law and had tried to kill him. He remembered the night of the attack by the lake and the horrific experience of almost drowning came back to him. Whatever happened, he was going to make sure that Lugg did not get away with it.

He had seen Lugg wheel away and ride back down the trail along which he and the rest of the gunnies had just come, and he began to work his way through the trees in that direction. There were open patches but he was well back from the trail and it was unlikely any of the gunslicks could see him. He began to move in an arc, which would bring him back out on the trail at a little further distance. The sounds of battle were loud and smoke drifted through the trees. At one point the roar of gunfire receded but it soon picked up again and he guessed that he was getting closer to the gunslicks' positions. He needed to be more cautious now and he crept forward slowly, glancing around him to guard against being taken by surprise.

Ahead of him was a thick tangle of brush. Suddenly a gun crashed; lead clipped a tree branch just above his head. Before the echoes had faded he threw himself to the ground. Pulling himself up onto one knee, he swung his rifle barrel up and around. Somebody was concealed in the brush. He shifted position slightly and glanced towards the nearest tree, contemplating making a run for it. He had some cover but he was still exposed. That fact was brought to his attention by the further bark of a gun, and a bullet slammed into the earth just ahead of him. As he cowered lower, a voice rang out.

'It ain't no use tryin' to make a run, Dwayne. I got you cold. Those two shots were just by way of bein' range finders. The next bullet is for you with my personal compliments.'

Dwayne recognized the voice. 'Lugg!' he snapped. His mind was working fast. Was it a coincidence that, of all the gunnies, it was Lugg he had stumbled across? More likely he and Lugg had had similar ideas and had been circling each other. The enmity which had grown up between them had become a personal affair even before this.

His leg was beginning to cramp and sweat had broken out on his forehead. He couldn't tell how much of him Lugg could see. He felt sure that if he attempted to move he would only expose himself more. Lugg was playing with him. As he shifted, his leg came in contact with something. He reached down; it was a windfall, a short tree branch. Almost without thinking, he quickly picked it up and with one movement lifted his arm and flung it away from him. As it crashed into the undergrowth there came a spurt of fire from the brush and a flash of flame as Lugg, taken by surprise, aimed a shot at where it had landed. The red fire indicated Lugg's position; in the second of time he had bought himself, Dwayne's rifle cracked and was answered with an unmistakable gasp of pain. Dwayne sprang to his feet and triggered a second shot. There was a muffled scream and then the brush parted and the figure of Lugg fell forward till the undergrowth stopped it. It sprawled, partly suspended, with its mouth open and its eyes staring skywards, like a broken doll.

Dwayne didn't lose any time; realizing that there might be other gunnies lurking nearby, he began to move quickly forward again, pushing through the tangled undergrowth. A little further along, the brush began to thin and, coming to an unexpected pile of rocks, he clambered up them. Just beyond, the scrub was thick but the crescendo of gunfire and the rising pall of smoke told him the gunnies had taken shelter there. He crouched low, scanning the scene in an attempt to locate where particular individuals might be located. Then he heard the snap of a twig behind him and spun round. Just emerging from a patch of brush was a man with his rifle raised. The man seemed to be unaware of his presence and Dwayne was just about to squeeze the trigger of his gun when he realized that it wasn't one of Tasker's gunslicks, but Brockley Whin.

Instead of firing, he raised his rifle above his head to attract Whin's attention. Whin came quickly forward.

'Dwayne,' he breathed. 'I guess you got the same idea as me.'

134

Dwayne wasn't certain what Whin meant and his lack of understanding must have been clear in his expression.

'To get behind the varmints,' Whin said.

'I came this way lookin' for Lugg,' the marshal responded.

Whin looked slightly bemused. 'Did you find him?' he asked.

'Yeah, I found him,' Dwayne replied.

'Thought I heard some shootin' close by,' Whin said. He still looked a little puzzled.

'My deputy,' Dwayne added. 'Remember? I figured there was somethin' wrong about him and I was right. He was ridin' with Tasker.'

Whin nodded; he vaguely recalled meeting the deputy after his release from jail but his focus now was on how to make best use of their position. He considered the situation for a few moments, looking all around as he did so.

'We could carry on further,' he said at length, 'but I don't think there'd be a lot of point. This seems to be the highest point and we got decent cover. I figure we could take on a whole bunch of Tasker's gun-hands right here.'

Dwayne saw the force of Whin's words and tried to put the last memory of Lugg out of his mind.

'Giroux and some of the Circle C men are back there. Maybe we could bring some of 'em up here.'

Whin shook his head. 'No time,' he replied. 'Tasker will probably have the same idea about tryin' to get behind us and besides, those boys have got their hands full already.'

'OK. So what do we do?'

'Load up,' Whin replied. 'We'll start shootin' and when we do those varmints are gonna start comin' right at us. That will be our chance.'

The marshal gave him a wry look. 'Our chance to be sittin' ducks,' he replied.

Whin grinned and started jamming slugs into his Winchester. Dwayne followed suit. When their rifles were ready they both checked their six-guns.

'OK,' Whin said. 'Are you ready?'

'It's been nice knowin' you,' Dwayne replied.

They each took up position and at a signal from Whin, opened fire on the position of the outlaws beneath them. There was a slight lull in the shooting, and then the fusillade was renewed, but this time it was aimed in their direction. At first the bullets flew harmlessly wide because the gunnies had not located the rocks behind which Whin and Dwayne were sheltering as the source of the attack, but they quickly realized the fact. Bullets began to whine overhead and ricochet among the rocks. Whin and Dwayne were well covered, however, and their ploy had its desired effect. They had a clearer idea now of the gunnies' locations and were confident that their fire was having some effect. Some of the gunslicks began to move and give away their positions, even unknowingly emerging from time to time into the open. Whin saw one man go down and then another and he had the impression that there was a lessening in the amount of fire being returned.

Suddenly a group of four gunnies appeared, running towards them. Whin had no idea what they were trying to achieve but they had made a bad mistake. Whin and Dwayne poured their fire on them and they went down in short order. At the same moment, bullets began to strike the rocks uncomfortably close and they realized that at least some of the gunnies had succeeded in getting close. Their position was becoming untenable.

'Time to move back!' Whin shouted. 'They're comin' in!'

He and Dwayne slid down the rocks into the cover of the bushes and began to work their way back in the direction of the line cabin. They moved quickly but, glancing back, Whin caught fleeting glimpses of figures moving among the trees and bushes. They were being pursued. Shots rang out at their rear but Whin was confident that they made a difficult target. They both staggered on and then, above the line of trees, they saw a plume of smoke. They burst through a patch of brush and saw the reason: the line cabin had been set alight. Flames were beginning to leap and dance and the plume of smoke soon became a gathering pall.

'I hope Crossan ain't in there!' Dwayne yelled.

As if in answer to his comment, a group of men appeared on the further side of the trail followed by two riders, who came galloping out of their midst towards Whin and Dwayne.

'What the—' Whin began, but before he could finish what he was saying, there was a cessation of shooting behind him, quickly followed by the sound of horses. He glanced round and caught a glimpse of riders heading quickly away and scattering in several directions. He looked up at the two horsemen coming from the direction of the line cabin and recognized them as Jubal and Jeb Crossan. One of them had a gun in his hand and was firing ahead; the other began to wave his arms and shout. Whin turned to Dwayne.

'I think we've got them on the run,' Dwayne said. 'I reckon Tasker has had enough. That's him and his men trying to get away.'

The group of men now came running up; Whin recognized them as Circle C hands. They were flushed with excitement. As they arrived, Underwood and some of the others who had taken up positions along the trail began to emerge from cover.

'By Jiminy,' one of the men said, 'we've got those varmints on the run!'

'What the hell are Jubal and Jeb doin'?' Whin said.

'There was no holdin' 'em back. Once we dealt with those gunnies back at the line cabin, he was for goin' after the rest of 'em.'

'Where's the doc?' Whin said.

'He's helpin' a couple of the boys that got wounded. He's OK.'

'You all got out of that burning building?' Dwayne snapped.

'Yeah. Leastways we did. I don't know about some of Tasker's men.'

Whin glanced up the trail, looking for Jubal and Jeb, but they had gone. The shooting had stopped and stray, frightened horses were wandering about, some of them saddled and others not. Two of them were standing nearby. Suddenly Whin ran to one of them and, seizing the bridle, calmed it down before leaping into the saddle.

'I'm goin' after Jubal and Jeb!' he shouted. 'The rest of you can follow later.'

He started along the trail in a cloud of dust. For a moment the others looked at one another in confusion till Underwood sprang to the other horse and hoisted himself into leather.

'Marshal, take care of things here!' he shouted. 'See how things are with the doc and the wounded men.'

'You be careful!' Dwayne replied.

139

Digging in his spurs, Underwood set off up the trail in pursuit of Whin and Tasker's beaten gang.

CHAPTER SEVEN

Whin rode hard and it wasn't long before he had caught up with Jubal and Jeb. They had been joined by Dunlop and Chet Hoover. Whin drew to a halt.

'They've scattered,' Jubal said.

Jeb let out a loud hoot. 'Man. We've sure taught them a lesson!' he exclaimed.

They heard approaching hoof beats and Underwood appeared. The mood was one of triumph but Whin was more restrained and interrupted the excited talk after a few minutes.

'We may have fought Tasker off,' he said, 'but he could still regroup. I figure we ain't done yet.'

Dunlop considered his words. 'Whin's right,' he said. 'This affair ain't over.'

'Tasker needs to be brought to justice,' Underwood said. 'He needs to answer for what he's done in a court of law.'

They looked at one another, uncertain of how to proceed. Finally Whin broke the silence.

'I reckon there ain't no time like the present,' he said. 'If we don't act now, we'll be handin' an invitation to Tasker to do this all over again. He'll have learnt from what happened today and he won't make the same mistakes again. He's gonna be more ruthless than ever the next time.'

'He's gonna be thirstin' for revenge,' Hoover interjected.

'So I say we finish this off here and now,' Whin said. 'What about the rest of you?'

'I'm with Whin,' Underwood said. 'I don't think we should wait.'

'What about the marshal and the rest of the men?' Hoover asked.

'The quicker we get on Tasker's trail the better,' Whin replied. 'It'll take up too much time to go back and round up the others.'

'There are six of us,' Jeb Crossan said. 'I figure that's more than enough.'

'Well said,' his father replied. 'Come on, then, what are we waitin' for?'

'You figure Tasker will head back for the Forked Lightning?' Underwood said, addressing Whin.

'Yeah, I reckon so. I don't know how many of the others will go with him. We could be in for a hot reception.'

'Let's go!' Jeb urged.

No one needed further persuasion. Without further discussion, they applied their spurs and set off for the Forked Lightning.

They rode hard. When they reached the gate with the Forked Lightning sign over it, there was no welcoming gunshot as there had been the first time Whin came by. All along the trail, however, there had been an abundance of sign and it was clear that a good number of Tasker's men had ridden back to the ranch, even if a lot of them had gone elsewhere.

'I sure hope Tasker's among them,' Jubal Crossan muttered.

Whin was hoping the same, but for different reasons. He had a sense of there being unfinished business between him and Tasker, which wasn't just to do with recent events at Blackwater and the Circle C.

They rode on. As they got near the Forked Lightning, they drew their rifles, ready for action. Whin's eyes were fixed on the trail ahead, expecting trouble at any moment. He was surprised that they had met with no opposition till he recalled that Tasker would have no reason to suppose that anyone would follow him. It was the one factor which gave them something of an edge. Even so, they would be well outnumbered. This time his keen eyes saw the tip of the windmill sails before they had a clear view of the ranch and he held up his hand to draw the others to a halt.

'The ranch house is just up ahead,' he said.

'OK,' Jubal replied. 'Let's go on in and get the varmints.' He couldn't conceal his eagerness to be up and at Tasker and his gunnies and the expression on his face was matched by that of his son. They were about to move off when Whin put out a hand to stop them.

'Just hold it a moment. Let's not get too excited. We don't want things to go off at half-cock.'

Jubal seemed about to object but then his fierce look softened. 'I guess you've got a point,' he said.

'We just need to give it a bit of thought,' Whin replied.

Underwood walked his horse forward a few paces and drew out a pair of field glasses he found in the saddle-bags. He put them to his eyes and surveyed the ranch house.

'I can't see any signs of activity,' he said. 'Here, someone else take a look.' He handed the glasses to Whin, who took a look before handing them on to Jubal Crossan.

'The sign leads right on down to the ranch,' Whin said. 'They've got to be there.'

'So what do we do?' Jubal said.

Whin had to admit that he was stumped. 'You wait here', he said to the others. 'I'll carry on and take a look.'

'No you won't,' Underwood said. 'We're in this together. If you go, we all go.'

Whin was about to argue the point but when he saw the grim, determined looks on his companions' faces, he knew that their minds were made up.

'Thanks,' he said. 'I guess I don't need to tell you to be careful.'

'We'll spread out,' Underwood added. 'That way we won't make so much of a target.'

'Have your rifles ready,' Whin said.

They moved forward again, drifting apart to form a line as Underwood suggested. As they rode, all their eyes were scanning the scene, alert to the merest suggestion of movement. It was easy to see where Tasker's men had ridden into the yard but as they got closer they could see that most of the tracks led beyond the ranch house in the direction of the stables. There seemed to be few boot prints in the dust. An uncanny quiet hung over the Forked Lightning. Only the creaking of the windmill disturbed the silence. They rode into the yard and Whin slipped from the saddle. Holding his Smith & Wesson No. 3 at the ready, he mounted the steps to the veranda and kicked at the door. It flew open and he dodged quickly inside. The room was empty. Quickly he glided to the stairs and ran up them. He passed down the passage, looking into the rooms, including the one in which he had previously stayed,

145

pausing long enough to glance out of the window. The place was deserted. Clattering down the stairs, he went back outside.

'There doesn't seem to be anyone here,' he said.

The others looked about them. Then Underwood suddenly clicked his fingers. 'I think I got it,' he said. 'Tasker must have realized Dwayne would soon be on his tail. Maybe not immediately, but pretty soon. He didn't want to take the chance of ending up behind bars. I figure him and his gunslicks have carried right on ridin'.'

There was a frustrated look on Jubal's face. 'Then where's he gone?' he asked.

There was a moment's silence and then Whin and Underwood exchanged glances as the same thought occurred to them both.

'Hell, I know,' Whin said. 'He's gone to join the rest of his boys on the trail drive. He's on his way to meet up with the herd.' He leaped back on his horse. 'It should be easy to carry on following the sign. He can't be too far ahead of us.'

When they rode out of the yard, it was immediately apparent that the trail led on beyond the stables and the outbuildings.

'Looks like we're right!' Dunlop shouted.

'We got him on the run!' Jeb exclaimed. 'He thinks he's got away, but he ain't!'

They rode hard for awhile till the horses began to

146

slow and they brought them down to a canter. As he rode, Whin found that something was troubling him. At first he tried to blot it out, but he found that he couldn't. It kept coming back. What was it? It was something to do with the ranch house. He thought back, going over the sequence of events. The door to the ranch house had been open. That was somewhat unusual in itself, but not sufficiently so to be what was bothering him. He had gone into the house and up the stairs to the bedrooms. He had looked out of the back window. There was something, but what? Then a vague impression began to rise towards the surface of his memory. His brain had barely registered the fact but there had been something in the lake. He still couldn't determine what it was but something told him that it was significant. Struggling to give a definite form to his shadowy intimations, he held up his arm as a signal to stop.

'What is it?' Jubal asked.

'I don't know. Somethin' back at the ranch.'

'What? We none of us saw anything.'

'I don't know,' Whin said, 'but I'm goin' back.'

'I'll come with you,' Underwood said.

'No,' Whin responded. 'It's probably nothin'. You boys carry on and I'll catch up with you.'

Underwood didn't look happy but the urgent voices of Jubal and Jeb were urging them onwards.

'Go on,' Whin said. 'I'll be back before you've

gone very far.' Without waiting for an answer, he turned the buckskin and started back up the trail. He glanced behind him to see that the others had started to ride on. Underwood hung back but after a few moments he carried on also.

It didn't take Whin long to arrive back at the ranch. Bypassing the windmill and the stables, he carried on to the lake shore where he halted the horse and jumped from the saddle. A wind had come up and was blowing mournfully through the reeds. He pushed forward till he had a view over the murky waters. At first he could see nothing and then his eyes detected something among the reeds at the edge of the water. He looked closely, squinting his eyes. Something told him what it was before he registered the fact. It was a body among the rushes at the margin of the water, moving gently as the waters lapped against the shore.

Whin shuddered. The wind was freshening and dark clouds had appeared, though which stabs of sunlight broke on the darkening waters. Little wavelets ran across and rippled in the sedge. He made his way round the edge of the lake to where the body lay, partly submerged. It was lying face down and he had to steel himself to bend and turn it over. It could only have been in the water a short time. The body was still fresh but Whin did not recognize the features. He had had a presentiment that it might be Tasker but it wasn't. Intrigued, he bent down again to take a closer look and instinctively, even before he heard the click of the catch on someone's rifle, he realized he was being careless. Too late he looked round. Amery Tasker had come up on him and was standing behind him with a Sharps .50 pointed at his head.

'I figured you'd be back,' Tasker said. His voice was strangely soft yet at the same time his words rang out clearly even above the soughing of the reeds in the wind.

'You figured right,' Whin replied. He started to turn round in order to face his former friend but Tasker's voice stopped him.

'I wouldn't make any sudden moves if I were you. Unfasten your gun-belt and throw it into the water.'

Even with his restricted vision, Whin realized that Tasker was just too far away for a sudden rush to carry any chance of success. One touch of Tasker's finger on the Sharps and his head would be blown off. Following Tasker's instructions to the letter, he undid his gun-belt and threw it into the gloomy waters of the lake. Even as he did so, and despite his desperate situation, he felt a tinge of regret at the loss of the new .44s.

'OK, Whin, you can turn round now.' Whin slowly did so. 'In case you're wonderin',' Tasker said, 'the man in the water is Nate Culver. He used to be my range boss. Not that that's likely to be of any interest to you.'

'You got a nice way of payin' him out,' Whin remarked.

'He'd have done better to have seen to the herd than come back here complainin'. Seemed he wasn't happy about some of the cattle carryin' a different brand.'

Tasker paused for a moment. Whin again considered the possibility of rushing him but rejected it.

'By the way,' Tasker continued, 'I presume you were behind that stampede caper. You shouldn't have interfered.'

'You were the one who sent for me,' Whin replied.

'I did, but I had something rather different in mind. I must say I've been rather disappointed in your response to my offer. I consider it was very generous. Thanks at least partly to you, I now find that my plans have had to be temporarily postponed.'

'You mean your plans to run some perfectly decent people off their land,' Whin replied. 'Your plans which included gunning down innocent people.'

'I take it you're referring to the Stamp Iron,' Tasker retorted. 'That was Baltimore Johnny's doing rather than mine. Perhaps he did go a little too far.'

'He was actin' on your orders,' Whin replied. 'What happened to you, Tasker? You used to be all right. When I heard you were lookin' for me and came out here, I didn't imagine there'd be anything like this.'

Tasker uttered a cynical laugh. 'You didn't expect me to be still punchin' cows? Obviously not. I guess that's where you and I differ, Whin. I guess that's why you're still ridin' the ranges and I got all this.' He jerked his head back in the direction of the Forked Lightning. 'I gave you credit for bein' more sensible. I figured you'd jump at the chance to hang up those guns. What have those stupid nesters ever done for you? You don't even know them.'

'I know them well enough,' Whin replied.

Tasker laughed again. 'I didn't figure you could be so stupid,' he said, 'but I should have known better. After all, you didn't show a lot of intelligence, even in the old days.'

'What do you mean?' Whin rapped.

'You probably thought I saved your neck when those jayhawkers were about to string you up. Hell, it was me set them onto you in the first place.'

Whin was struggling to understand what Tasker was saying. 'What do you mean? Are you tryin' to tell me you set me up?'

'Let me recall the circumstances. We'd driven a herd up to Baxter Springs. You might recall that Robertson, the trail boss, came to a sticky end not long before we reached it.'

151

'He got trampled. It was an accident.'

'It weren't no accident. Let's say he stopped a bullet not long before that happened.'

'You mean, you fixed it so that it looked like he got trampled? You killed him?'

'You're beginning to catch on. Let's just say I had an alternative arrangement regarding the sale of those beeves. I guess it was about that time I began to realize that punchin' cows was a loser's game. Makin' a big profit and keepin' it for myself kinda proved that I was right.'

'I still don't get it,' Whin said.

'It really isn't that hard. You and Robertson seemed to get on pretty well. I figured you were suspicious. I arranged for some of those jayhawkers to catch up with you. Then I figured I could do even better by comin' to your rescue. That way I'd throw you off the scent and avoid any possible trouble with the farmers. They might have taken it into their heads to take the whole affair one step further. Either that or the rest of the boys in the outfit might have decided to go out lookin' for revenge. Either way, it could have upset my plans.'

'You worked both sides of the fence,' Whin said. 'You were in with the jayhawkers.'

'Sure. I knowed some of 'em from the War years; even fought alongside 'em.'

'You two-faced scum,' Whin said.

Tasker laughed once more but this time there was an even more menacing edge to it.

'I'd be careful what I was sayin' if I were you,' he snarled. 'Fact of the matter is, it didn't matter to me which side was which or what the rights and wrongs of it all were. Hell, what did I care? Those farmers, those cowmen, what difference did it make to me? The only thing I was concerned about was makin' sure I came out of it on top.'

'So nothin's changed,' Whin replied.

'You were a fool then and you are now,' Tasker said. 'I gave you a chance and you rejected it.'

'Somebody asked me what had happened to make you the way you are,' Whin replied. 'I can see now that nothin' happened. You were always the same. You were scum then and you're scum now.'

Tasker's face was grim. Even in the fading light, Whin could see a nerve twitch in his cheek. He had lowered the Sharps but now he raised it again.

'I've had about enough of this,' he said. 'Face it, Whin. You made a bad choice, a real bad choice. And now you're gonna find out just how bad.'

'It was you who made the wrong choice,' Whin retorted, 'when you decided to send for me. You figured because I had a reputation with a gun that I was like you. But I'm not like you.' He looked down at the body lying in the water. 'He's the one who's like you. You're a dead man, Tasker, dead to the core,

153

and by your own decision.'

While they were talking, Whin had imperceptibly changed his position. The sun was sinking low in the sky behind him and when it broke through the clouds it would be in Tasker's eyes. He was waiting for the right moment. Tasker's face was set in a wolfish snarl as he spat out his final words.

'Just remember, Whin, it could have been different.'

He raised the Sharps. At the same moment the sun broke through. Without hesitation Whin flung himself forward. He heard the boom of the gun and the crump of the bullet as it flew past his head. He was doubled over and the next moment his head crashed into Tasker's midriff. The Sharps exploded again but the bullet flew harmlessly into the air. The shock of the impact tore the rifle from Tasker's hands as he staggered back under the impact of Whin's assault. He quickly recovered his equilibrium, however, and as Whin straightened up, he kicked out, catching Whin's leg. Whin went down and as he attempted to roll clear, Tasker came in with a kick to the chest. Whin felt a sharp pain but Tasker had been off-balance and the blow didn't land with its full force.

As Tasker lunged in again, Whin kicked out and Tasker stumbled. Whin scrambled to his feet and as Tasker regained his balance, managed to land a sharp blow which split Tasker's lip. Tasker paused, putting the back of his hand to his bloody mouth. The next moment his hand began to fall towards his holster but Whin was too quick and before he could draw his six-gun, Whin came in and smashed a right-hander to Tasker's chin. Tasker stumbled back but Whin was careless and as he swung again, Tasker ducked under his arm and butted him in the belly. Whin gasped as the air was driven out of him but he succeeded in backing off just long enough to give him a vital moment's respite.

Tasker stepped forward again but Whin side-stepped his rush and caught him with a swinging punch to the back of the head. Before Tasker could recover, Whin stepped in with a quick right and left to the face. Tasker started to fall and as he did so, Whin responded with a swinging uppercut, which he aimed at Tasker's chin but which caught him in the windpipe. Tasker reeled, gasping for breath, and Whin, seizing his advantage, came in with a shudder-ing blow to the kidney. Tasker straightened, his face twisted in pain, as Whin smashed a blow to his chin. This time it landed; Whin heard a cracking sound as Tasker's head jerked back and then he crumpled to the ground like a discarded dummy. He lay unmov-ing. Whin put his hands on his hips to get his breath back before bending down over the inert body. A glance was enough to tell him that Tasker's jaw was broken. He lay unconscious, his body twisted with one arm caught underneath him.

Whin sank to the ground, and as he did so he heard a loud explosion. For an instant his befuddled senses did not register what had happened but as another report rang out and something whizzed by his head, he realized that he was under fire. He heard the sound of running feet and looked up to see someone coming towards him with a rifle in his hands. He was closing fast and Whin was unarmed. The man's next bullet could hardly fail to find its target. Acting on some kind of urgent instinct, Whin reached down for Tasker's holster. In one swift, fluid movement Tasker's gun was in his hand and spitting lead. The man stopped in his tracks. Whin's gun spoke again but the man remained standing. Slowly he raised his rifle but before his finger could close on the trigger he fell face-forward into the mud.

Whin remained crouching for a few moments and then rose to his feet. His eyes swept the lakeside but there was nothing to be seen. The dwindling sun had disappeared behind some clouds and darkness was sweeping over the lake. A menacing wind whispered through the reeds. Whin walked slowly to where the newcomer lay, his body riddled with bullets. Whin's path had once crossed that of the man lying dead at his feet. In any event he would have been certain by his unmarked, weasel-like features that the man he had shot was Baltimore Johnny. He turned and began to walk away from the lakeside, the sinking sun at his back. The buckskin was standing where he had left it. Wearily, he climbed into the saddle and began to ride away from the Forked Lightning.

A little more than a week had passed and the Circle C was buzzing with anticipation. The yard was crowded with people. The stables were filled with horses and a variety of rigs were lined up beside the corrals. It seemed that most of the population of Blackwater had come to see if Jeb Crossan would make it back to the ranch carrying his new bride. He had carried her from the church where they had been married earlier that afternoon almost as far as the old oak grove but special arrangements had been made for him to complete the required distance by finishing at the ranch house. From inside the building the sound of fiddles and the responsive shuffle of feet emerged and young men with their girls passed in and out through the open door. Brockley Whin was standing in a little circle of people which included Underwood, Giroux and Doc Smith.

'Whether Jeb makes it or not,' Underwood said, 'at least we don't have to worry about him bein' dry-gulched this time.' Giroux looked slightly concerned.

'There are folks at different points all along the route,' the doctor commented.

'More to the point,' Whin replied, 'the marshal has Tasker under lock and key and his gang of gunslicks are either right there alongside him or long gone.'

Underwood turned to him. 'I still feel kinda bad about leavin' you to ride on back to the Forked Lightning,' he said. 'Things could have turned out a whole lot different than they did.'

'You and the others did the right thing to carry on,' Whin replied. 'You did a great job of roundin' up the rest of those gunnies. The ones who got away ain't ever likely to come by this way again.'

'All the same, I ought to have gone to the Forked Lightning with you.'

'I only went back on a hunch,' Whin replied. 'Like I say, you all did right. Things have turned out fine.'

'I still don't understand what Baltimore Johnny was doing back there,' the doctor said.

'I reckon him and Tasker were aimin' to lie low till things blew over a bit,' Whin replied. 'They probably figured the best thing was to hide out around the Forked Lightning and see what developed. When the trail hands got back with the money, they probably figured they could soon get a new bunch of gunhawks together.'

'Once those cowpokes got to learn what happened to their trail boss, I doubt whether they'd have had any truck with Tasker,' Underwood said.

'Maybe not. I guess we'll never know. But Tasker

was certainly not expectin' Nate Culver to turn up at the Forked Lightning.'

'Nate was a good man,' the doctor said. 'I figure he was wise to what was going on.'

'It ain't any sort of consolation,' Giroux said, 'but it was Whin seeing him in the lake that led to Tasker's final downfall.'

'Tasker deserves to hang,' Underwood muttered. 'And I guess he probably will once the circuit judge comes to town.'

Suddenly their conversation was broken into by the sound of cheering. They turned their heads and there, coming into view, was the figure of young Jeb Crossan carrying Willow Giroux in his arms. A look of triumph had spread across his features. His father, Jubal, was just behind, shouting words of encouragement. The doctor turned to the others.

'I figured that boy would do it,' he said.

'Who wouldn't with a girl like that,' Whin replied. Jeb walked into the yard where he finally put his burden down.

'Well done, son,' Jubal said. His words were drowned as people cheered and shouted and a voice rose above the tumult:

'Ain't you gonna kiss the bride?'

Jeb looked a little sheepish but then took Willow in his arms and they engaged in a long kiss.

'Guess they'll be carrryin' each other from now

159

on,' Giroux remarked.

The young couple moved into the house with their supporters in their wake. Whin looked across the room, full of excited talk and busy movement, and saw the person he was looking for. She was wearing a simple, plain blouse and skirt and she had put her hair up. The room had been cleared and the first couples were stepping onto the floor for a new set of dancing. Coloured lanterns shed a warm glow and streamers hung from the ceiling. The fiddlers were getting ready to strike up a tune when Whin got next to Etta Foy.

'Would you give me the honour of the next dance?' he said.

She looked at him with warm, gentle eyes and nodded. He took her hand and they joined the waiting dancers. The music started. He put his hand around her waist and they glided off together. Whin felt the warmth of her close to him, breathed in the scent of her hair and knew he had been right to come to Blackwater.

Underwood and the marshal, standing at the edge of the dance floor, exchanged glances.

'I figure it ain't only Jubal Crossan takin' him on at the Circle C that's gonna keep Whin in Blackwater,' the marshal commented.

Underwood grinned. 'I think things are gonna be a lot different at the Black Cat from now on,' he replied.